I closed my eyes again, squeezing them shut as I ordered my brain to cease and desist with disquiet and unrest. Sleep was what I needed. Tranquility was what I craved. Peace was what I deserved.

A rasping sound from the opposite side of the cabin caught my ears, and I turned my head toward the noise. Yellow flickering light fell across my silvery-streaked cabin as the door opened. The door creaked on its hinges.

I muffled a shriek behind my hand and froze.

"Good night, Mr. Graham," a man said.

"Good night, sir," another male voice echoed.

The man called "sir" stepped into the room, and the door closed behind him, darkening the room once again to a sliver of moonlight. The yellow light had disappeared. I held my breath, unsure what to do.

Clearly the man had entered the wrong cabin, though I had no idea how he had managed to use his key card to enter my room. I knew I ought to jump out of bed and run the intruder out of my cabin, but I remained frozen under the covers. My heart pounded. I waited, as curious as I was frightened.

"Sir" bumped into something and emitted a soft curse.

"Drat!"

A Ship Through Time

Bess McBride

A Ship Through Time

Copyright 2017 Bess McBride

Contact information: bessmcbride@gmail.com

Cover art by Tara West
Interior formatting by Author E.M.S.

ISBN-13: 978-1546315896
ISBN-10: 1546315896

Published in the United States of America

Books by Bess McBride

Time Travel Romance

The Highlander's Stronghold
(Book One of the Searching for a Highlander series)

My Laird's Castle
(Book One of the My Laird's Castle series)

My Laird's Love
(Book Two of the My Laird's Castle series)

My Laird's Heart
(Book Three of the My Laird's Castle series)

Caving in to You
(Book One of the Love in the Old West series)

A Home in Your Heart
(Book Two of the Love in the Old West series)

Forever Beside You in Time

Moonlight Wishes in Time
(Book One of the Moonlight Wishes in Time series)

Under an English Moon
(Book Two of the Moonlight Wishes in Time series)

Following You Through Time
(Book Three of the Moonlight Wishes in Time series)

A Train Through Time
(Book One of the Train Through Time series)

Together Forever in Time
(Book Two of the Train Through Time series)

A Smile in Time
(Book Three of the Train Through Time series)

Finding You in Time
(Book Four of the Train Through Time series)

A Fall in Time
(Book Five of the Train Through Time series)

Train Through Time Series Boxed Set
(Books 1-3)

Across the Winds of Time

A Wedding Across the Winds of Time

Love of My Heart

Historical Romance

Anna and the Conductor

The Earl's Beloved Match

Short Cozy Mysteries by Minnie Crockwell

Will Travel for Trouble Series

Trouble at Happy Trails *(Book 1)*

Trouble at Sunny Lake *(Book 2)*

Trouble at Glacier *(Book 3)*

Trouble at Hungry Horse *(Book 4)*

Trouble at Snake and Clearwater *(Book 5)*

Trouble in Florence *(Book 6)*

Trouble in Tombstone Town *(Book 7)*

Trouble in Cochise Stronghold *(Book 8)*

Trouble in Orange Beach *(Book 9)*

Trouble at Pelican Penthouse *(Book 10)*

DEDICATION

To my little girl
I wish you could have been with me.
We would have had a great time!

To Cousin Margaret Wollam
I wish you could have been with me too.
I think of you.

Dear Reader,

Thank you for purchasing *A Ship Through Time*. *A Ship Through Time* was inspired by my love of cruising and the South Pacific. What better way to celebrate both than by combining them into a time travel romance? Who knows—the Caribbean might be next!

Here's a bit about the story.

Maggie Wollam embarks on a cruise to the South Pacific on the two-year anniversary of her husband's death—in the twenty-first century. When she awakens aboard a ship in the nineteenth century, she assumes she's dreaming. Even the handsome ship's doctor can't convince her that she must have traveled through time.

Dr. Daniel Hawthorne doesn't know what to do with the odd woman who keeps materializing out of thin air and then vanishing from his cabin. How long can he hide her from the captain, the crew, the other passengers? But hiding his time traveler hardly seems to matter when the ship flounders during a storm somewhere in the South Pacific.

Can Maggie travel back through time to save herself? Would she leave Daniel if she could?

Thank you for your support over the years, friends and readers. Because of your favorable comments, I continue to strive to write the best stories I can. More romances are on the way!

You know I always enjoy hearing from you, so please feel free to contact me at bessmcbride@gmail.com or through my website at http://www.bessmcbride.com.

Many of you know I also write a series of short cozy mysteries under the pen name of Minnie Crockwell. Feel free to stop by my website and learn more about the series.

Thanks for reading!

Bess

CHAPTER ONE

Leaving the balcony door of my aft-facing cabin open, I crawled into bed. I rolled over onto my back and listened to the hum of the massive turbines far below intermingled with the hypnotic hiss of waves as the ship cleaved through the Pacific Ocean. The sweet-salty smell of fresh sea air acted as a relaxing sedative, and I imagined I was being treated to a soothing massage in the *Century Star*'s spa.

The combination of rhythmic sound and delicate fragrance lulled me into a state of drowsiness, and I closed my eyes. But as had become a habit of late, the moment between drowsiness and sleep seemed to elude me, and within minutes, I heaved a sigh and opened my eyes.

An echo of moonlight peeked in through several portholes, sending soft silver streaks throughout the cabin. I turned my head toward the portholes, wondering why I hadn't noticed them upon boarding the ship only hours before. That a balcony cabin would also feature the small circular windows along the same wall surprised me. Oddly, I couldn't make out the outline of the balcony door.

I flipped onto my side to face the portholes and watched moonlight bobbing in and out of sight as the ship rose and fell over the waves. Why I had recently begun to struggle with insomnia was beyond me. No, that wasn't quite true. I had concerns. I had fears. I had angst. Life had handed me lemons, and they were bitter.

I closed my eyes again, squeezing them shut as I ordered my brain to cease and desist with disquiet and unrest. Sleep was what I needed. Tranquility was what I craved. Peace was what I deserved.

A rasping sound from the opposite side of the cabin caught my ears, and I turned my head toward the noise. Yellow flickering light fell across my silvery-streaked cabin as the door opened. The door creaked on its hinges.

I muffled a shriek behind my hand and froze.

"Good night, Thomas," a man said.

"Good night, sir," another younger male voice echoed.

The man called "sir" stepped into the room, and the door closed behind him, darkening the space once again to a sliver of moonlight. The yellow light had disappeared. I held my breath, unsure what to do.

Clearly, the man had entered the wrong cabin, though I had no idea how he had managed to use his key card to enter my room. I knew I ought to jump out of bed and run the intruder out of my cabin, but I remained frozen under the covers. My heart pounded. I waited, as curious as I was frightened.

"Sir" bumped into something and emitted a soft curse.

"Drat!"

My eyes having adjusted to the darkness longer than Sir's, I rather thought I could see him better than he could see me, and I was surprised to see the tall man throw a wheel hat onto a chair, as if he knew his way around the cabin. The white-capped, dark-brimmed hat resembled those I had seen on ships' officers. Given the monochromatic tones of the room lit only by moonlight, I wondered if the light stripes across the bottom of Sir's sleeves were of gold braid, like an officer's insignia.

He unbuttoned a double-breasted dark jacket and carelessly tossed it onto the same chair holding his hat. In white shirtsleeves, he shrugged out of dark suspenders, loosened a necktie and began to unbutton his shirt.

It wasn't until after Sir had slipped out of his shirt and sat down on the end of the bed, as if to remove his shoes, that I decided to put a halt to the proceedings.

"Before you go any further," I began, "you should know that you're in the wrong cabin."

Sir cursed again as he jumped up from the bed and spun around to look at me. I barely had time to wriggle into a sitting position and pull the covers to my chest as he reached for something on a nearby table. A lantern came alive with a yellow hazy glow.

"What the devil?" he said. Blue-black, well-groomed hair ending just below his ears gleamed in the favorable soft lighting. Thick dark eyebrows narrowed as he stared at me. A cleft in his chin deepened with his frown.

"Who are you?" he barked in a full baritone.

I would have answered, but I was stunned to see the cabin transformed. Gone were the television and compact refrigerator from the opposite wall. Gone was the comfortable cloth sofa along that same wall. The mirror, which had flanked one wall of the cabin, had been replaced by a small picture frame–sized mirror. The festively striped balcony curtains of blue and green were gone.

"What on earth?" I muttered. Even the gray quilt I hugged to my chest bore no resemblance to the cream-colored duvet I had slid beneath only moments before. The furnishings in the room were sparse, of dark wood and without upholstering.

"I ask you again, madam, who are you, and what are you doing in my cabin? I do not know what you think you are about, but I'll have none of this nonsense. If this is someone's idea of a jest, they will be sorely disappointed. I am not amused."

He might as well have said "we" are not amused, so arrogant was his tone.

"A jest?" I stuttered on the words. "This is *my* cabin." My tone was defiant, but I had begun to doubt my words. How could the completely transformed cabin have been mine?

"That is simply not possible. This is my cabin," he said. "Where did you come from? I have not seen you on the ship before."

"Seattle," I said. "Well, I flew into San Francisco to catch the cruise, but Seattle. I'm from Seattle," I rambled.

Sir stared at me for a moment, as if I were an alien, before turning to look at the door. He shook his head and returned his attention to me.

"Have you stowed away? Is it possible? I have met all the passengers on this voyage. There are only a handful."

"Stowed away? No! This is *my* cabin!"

He put his hands on his hips and stared at me for a moment. I was no longer sure he had walked into the wrong cabin, but I didn't know what to think. I scanned the room again. No, the small wooden desk had not been there. The wooden chairs? No.

"Come now, madam! Rise from the bed and dress yourself. You cannot stay here. Even if you have stowed away, there is nothing to be done about your presence now, but you cannot stay in my cabin. I will have the cabin boy find other quarters for you."

I didn't budge but bunched the covers around my throat.

Sir waited with an expectant lift of his eyebrows. He seemed disinclined to snatch me up from the bed.

"Madam?" he prompted.

"I don't know where my clothes are," I said feebly. The closet where I'd hung my clothes had vanished. I wore only a cotton shorty nightgown.

Sir drew in a sharp breath and scanned the cabin, as if looking for my clothes.

"No, don't bother. You're not going to find them," I said.

"I beg your pardon?"

"They're not going to be here. I'm probably in a dream, so why would I think to bring extra clothes, right?"

I had decided in the last few seconds that I had to be in a dream. There could be no other explanation. Clearly I was no longer in my original cabin, and I didn't have a habit of sleepwalking. Nor did the stark cabin I now sat in resemble anything on a modern cruise ship. Even the vague creaking sounds of the ship and significant swaying seemed jarring.

Sir's jaw slackened as he drew in another breath. I imagined he didn't often look so stumped. My initial impression was that he was a decisive man, a figure of authority, a bit solemn. I wondered if he smiled easily. I suspected not.

One small superficial, foolish part of my brain tried not to take offense at the fact that Sir seemed so eager to get rid of me. I was, after all, a fairly young twenty-five year-old woman lying in his bed. A quick check of his ring finger showed no wedding band. I didn't think I was any great shakes, but there I was, and the handsome ship's officer was only too eager to get rid of me.

I realized the absurdity of my thoughts and put a quick stop to them. The sight of a partially undressed man in my cabin late at night aboard a cruise to the South Pacific was obviously heady stuff. I'd been ripe for such romantic yearnings, and my imagination had come through.

"You have no clothing at all, madam?" he repeated in an incredulous tone. "But how did you board the ship? Certainly not in a state of undress." He stepped forward to the end of the bed. "Were you spirited aboard? Kidnapped? Who among the crew would do such a thing? Name the lout!"

A lout?

"No louts," I mumbled. "No, I don't think I was kidnapped. The last thing I remember is going to sleep...in another cabin."

"I see. Then perhaps you *are* one of our guests after all." The creases in his tanned brow relaxed. Until he scrunched his forehead again. "Yet I have met both of the ladies traveling with us on this voyage, Mrs.

Simpson and Mrs. Darymple. Mrs. Simpson is acting as maid and companion to Mrs. Darymple. I am not aware of any other passengers of the feminine persuasion."

Feminine persuasion?

"Well, apparently you have a third lady traveling with you now. Where are we going, by the way?"

He blinked and ran a hasty hand across his chin, as if to stall.

"No, I am not convinced. I think I must ask again. Did someone bring you aboard without the captain's permission? Even if I could imagine such a foul deed, why would they stow you in *my* cabin, of all places?" He shook his head. "No, that simply does not make sense. None of the crew would have brought you aboard or deposited you in my room. I am stymied."

"Me too," I said, enjoying his old-fashioned use of the English language. "Stymied, that is. So where did you say we were going? I was on my way to the South Pacific, to the Tahitian Islands."

I had relaxed, though I still kept the covers pressed up against my chin. Secure in the knowledge that I was dreaming, I determined to see the dream through. I think I would much rather have ended up in Sir's embrace rather than this repudiation of my presence, but could one really control dreams?

"Yes, that is correct. Tahiti."

Sir braced his hands on his hips again and studied me.

"I apologize if I seem rude, madam, but your presence has taken me by surprise. And your circumstances lend an even greater challenge. You say you have no clothing. Therefore, I cannot simply willy-nilly remove you from my quarters. You need clothing. And we must find a spare cabin for you. All without the captain's knowledge, for he will surely have two of his burliest sailors deposit you on the next wharf regardless of your present state of undress."

"Sure," I purred, amused at his discomfiture. My original anxiety had given way to an odd sort of tranquility as I watched the events in my dream unfold.

He eyed me suspiciously before rebuttoning his shirt and slipping his suspenders over his shoulders again.

"I shall have to rely upon my cabin steward's discretion. Thomas is a good lad, resourceful. Please wait here."

"I'm not going anywhere...for now." I grinned, and Sir blinked, shook his head and turned for the door.

"Hey, what's your name, by the way?" I called out.

He turned back and bowed at the waist.

"Introductions, yes, of course," he intoned unenthusiastically. "I suppose we should. I am Dr. Daniel Hawthorne, ship's doctor of the *Vigilance*. And you are?"

"Margaret Wollam. Most people call me Maggie."

"I wish that I could say it was a pleasure to meet you, Miss Wollam, but under the circumstances—" Dr. Hawthorne stopped. "That is to say, I am not displeased precisely. Well, no, I *am* displeased actually, but I think I must stop speaking, for I am making a great mess of it." He rolled his dark eyes almost comically, and I had the distinct impression that the good doctor was as shy as he was solemn.

"Is it *Mrs.* Wollam? Or Miss Wollam?"

"Mrs. Wollam, actually," I said. "I'm a widow."

"So young!" he murmured. "My condolences," he said with a brief bow.

"Thank you," I responded quietly. Determined to do nothing to draw myself out of the dream, I said nothing further about my past.

Daniel rubbed his hands together.

"Very well then. I will return in a moment."

"Okay, hurry back!"

He stopped in midstride and turned back to look at me with a startled expression. I gave him a foolish grin before he turned to leave.

Left alone, a quick study of the cabin confirmed again that it looked nothing like the one I'd been using for the past eight days since we'd left San Francisco.

With one eye on the door, I slipped out of bed, straightened my nightgown and crossed the cabin to look out one of the portholes, surprised that the doctor didn't rate a balcony. The moon glowed on the sea, spreading a lovely white sheen across the darkness.

The door behind me opened much sooner than I anticipated, and I scurried back across the room and jumped into bed.

Daniel coughed and turned his back.

"Forgive me. I did not realize you were up and about. I should have knocked but am not used to doing so in my own cabin. May I turn?"

"Sure," I said, my cheeks hot with a flush. My light-blue nightgown covered me adequately, but something in the doctor's tone made me blush. Maybe he didn't treat women in his practice?

"Thomas is preparing a cabin for you. He informed me that we have no vacant passenger cabins, so he has offered his cabin. He shares it with another steward, but they will bunk with the rest of the crew.

"Thomas will fetch some tea to your cabin shortly. Frankly, we were not able to devise a scheme to obtain proper ladies' clothing for you, but I will give that some further thought. Until I do arrive at a solution, you must stay in your cabin, Mrs. Wollam."

I was about to protest but thought better of it as I watched Daniel cross over to a trunk at the foot of the bed and retrieve what looked like a red velvet robe. If I protested, he might lock me in the cabin. If I kept quiet, he might leave the door open, and I could explore the ship.

Daniel handed me the robe and turned his back. "If you would be so good as to don my robe, I will escort you to Thomas's cabin."

I slipped out of bed and wrapped the robe around me. The hem dusted the floor, and the sleeves fell below my hands. At about six-feet-two-inches, Daniel was a foot taller than me.

"Okay," I said.

Daniel turned around, and attempting to avert his eyes, he picked up the oil lantern before leading the way to the door. Easing it open, he peered into the hallway and stepped out. He signaled me forward and put a cautionary finger to his lips.

I stepped out into the hall. Much narrower than the *Century Star*, the hall featured one dimly lit sconce and a well-worn strip of dark-red nondescript carpet. I followed Daniel down the hallway.

He stopped at a wooden stairwell, and we descended to the next deck. The faded carpeting above gave way to varnished wood flooring that showed heavy use. In bare feet, I rose up on my toe tips to avoid the cold surface as I continued to follow Daniel. He stopped in front of a plain heavy wooden door and pushed it open, allowing me to enter first.

After a moment's hesitation, I entered the cabin. A wall sconce flickered, shedding faint yellow light onto the room. Daniel's sparse cabin seemed luxurious compared to the Spartan furnishings and miniscule size of the stewards' hovel. Two short wooden bunks had been jammed rather than built into one nook. A small wooden locker, desk and chair dominated another wall. The scratched and dented desk featured a dingy ceramic bowl and pitcher.

"I'd rather have your cabin," I muttered, staring at the cold wooden flooring under my toes. Daniel stepped in and maneuvered past me in the tiny cabin to set his oil lantern down on the desk. He put his hands on his hips to survey the area, the gesture seeming to take up any remaining space.

"I apologize for the austere conditions, but we have only a few passenger cabins, and as I said, those are occupied. I could not place you in crew quarters, and Thomas did relinquish his cabin to you. The other steward does not know why he was forced to move."

I realized Daniel thought I was ungrateful, and he was right. I wasn't happy. What a depressing dream! My hero had been unhappy to see me, greeting me not with passion and romance but as an unwelcome intrusion, a stowaway.

I had no complaints about his looks though. He was as handsome as any hero I could have imagined with dark wavy hair, nut-brown eyes and a cleft chin.

"I'm grateful to Thomas," I said dutifully. I wasn't in the least, but I couldn't very well say so.

At a tap on the door, Daniel put his finger to his lips again, and I bit my lip as he eased open the door. A creak from ungreased hinges thwarted his attempts at stealth. He stood back and allowed a pint-sized teenage boy carrying a tray with a plain white porcelain tea set to enter the room. Probably about seventeen, Thomas wore a misbuttoned dark jacket and brown trousers. His rumpled short blond hair suggested Daniel had roused him from sleep, though the bunks appeared neatly made with gray blankets.

The boy's blue eyes widened when he saw me. He set the tray down on the desk beside the lamp and turned toward Daniel, throwing glances my way out of the corner of his eye.

"Will there be anything else, Doctor?"

"No, Thomas. Thank you. Please bring Mrs. Wollam some breakfast in the morning."

"Aye, sir," Thomas said, touching a finger to his forehead in a small salute. He threw one more look at me over his shoulder as he left the room.

I turned and sat down on the edge of the bottom bunk.

"Please do not leave the cabin, Mrs. Wollam, until we can find you some proper clothing. I shall return in the morning. I trust you have everything you need for the evening?"

I quirked an eyebrow. Surely Daniel wasn't really leaving. He wasn't actually planning to leave me in the closet-cabin, was he?

"That's it?" I asked.

Daniel had picked up the lantern and turned for the door but stopped and pivoted when I spoke.

"I beg pardon?"

"Are you really just going to leave me here?"

"Yes, of course, Mrs. Wollam. What else would I do with you?"

Daniel's tanned cheeks bronzed, and my own face flamed. Didn't people normally skip all the awkwardness of life in dreams?

"This is about the most unromantic dream I could have imagined," I muttered.

"Ro...romantic?" Daniel stammered. "Good gravy, Mrs. Wollam, whatever can you be thinking?"

"Well, if I'm dreaming, why would I stick myself away in this microscopic hamster cage on a ship bound for Tahiti? What kind of a dream is that?"

"You are not dreaming, Mrs. Wollam. This is as far from a dream as *I* can possibly imagine!"

CHAPTER TWO

I opened my eyes and looked around the room. Light peeked in through the blue-and-green curtains of the balcony, allowing me to see that I was in my cabin on the *Century Star*.

I hopped out of bed and ran to the curtains to draw them apart. Sunlight streamed into the cabin. The events of the previous night had truly been nothing but a dream.

A knock on the door startled me. Daniel? Thomas? I ran for the door, almost expecting to see one of them, but the sight of the young dark-haired room service attendant convinced me that I was fully awake and in the present. Dressed in a trim black coat, matching trousers and clean white shirt, the waiter bid me good morning as he delivered my breakfast on a stainless-steel tray.

He set the tray down on the tiny round coffee table in the cabin, and I looked for my purse to find tip money. I realized at that moment that I was still in my nightgown, but the room service waiter hardly seemed to notice. Accepting the tip with a bow, he left after wishing me a good day, and I sank down onto a chair in front of the food, eyeing the oatmeal, fruit, coffee and juice without really seeing it.

What a terribly unsatisfactory dream! I felt cheated. Not only had it been extremely odd and not a little unpleasant, I had awakened somewhere in the middle of the dream. Surely Daniel's final frustrated words as he prepared to leave me in a tiny crew cabin couldn't have been the end of the dream.

You are not dreaming, Mrs. Wollam. This is as far from a dream as I can possibly imagine!

I'd wanted to tell Daniel that it hadn't been *my* idea to dream myself into his cabin, that if *I'd* had my way, he would have been happy to see me in his bed.

I picked at my breakfast, trying to dispel the remnants of the strange dream by reviewing the ship's daily calendar. An at-sea day, the program showed a myriad of activities, which I normally sampled. Unable to shake my sense of dissatisfaction though, I tossed the program aside and finished my breakfast.

I showered, dressed and headed out to stroll on the promenade deck. My fellow walkers passed me easily, desperately trying to work off the calories of the plentiful free meals offered by the ship.

When the combination of fresh sea air and light exercise failed to ease my restlessness, I made my way to the computer room to dash off a few e-mails to several friends and my mother-in-law.

Like me, Kathy suffered during November, the month my husband died two years ago of an aneurysm. Jeff had been her only son, and my heart went out to her. My husband and I hadn't even managed to provide her with a grandchild in our short two-year marriage. We had been thinking about starting a family but hadn't yet conceived when Jeff died unexpectedly.

His life insurance had left me well provided for, and I made an additional living painting. I had sold a few pieces here and there, mostly Pacific coastal scenes near my home in Washington state, and I had hoped to lighten my canvas and include some works in Pacific island colors.

I had deliberately booked a monthlong cruise to the South Pacific to get away from my grief and to immerse myself in something that didn't remind me of Jeff.

Oddly, I'd had no dreams since Jeff died, not until the previous night. One would have thought that if I was going to finally dream—and remember it in vivid detail—the dream would have eased my loneliness, not added to it. Dr. Daniel Hawthorne, stern and unyielding, the complete opposite of my sociable easygoing blond husband, had definitely not welcomed me into his world, and I felt lonelier than ever.

I returned to my cabin and stepped out onto my balcony. Warm salty air blew through my shoulder-length hair, relaxing me, enveloping me in its sweet humidity. I sat down in one deck chair and propped my feet up on the other. The gentle sway of the ship lulled me into a state of drowsiness, and I closed my eyes.

"Did I not expressly forbid you to leave the cabin?" a harsh male voice spoke near my ear.

I popped open my eyes and bolted upright. Seated not on my balcony but in a wooden chair somewhere on the deck of a creaking ship, I looked up to see Dr. Daniel Hawthorne, now resplendent in his black uniform. Brass double-breasted jacket buttons complemented the gold braid on his sleeves. At present, he wore his wheel hat, and he looked unbearably handsome. However, the dark glare he directed at me from under the shiny black visor unnerved me.

He had whispered into my ear and now straightened. I looked down at my clothing, startled to see that I wore nothing but my short cotton nightgown. I couldn't blame him. I was largely undressed and apparently sitting on the upper deck of the *Vigilance*.

I jumped up.

"I'm back!" I whispered.

"You never left," Daniel muttered. He took me by the arm, forcefully but without pain, and he maneuvered me through a nearby wooden door. Just as the door shut behind us, I saw two women come around the corner, promenading in fabulous costumes from a historical era. Their blousy sleeves, tightly corseted waists and broad skirts reminded me of Victorian-era dresses. Dark bonnets and draping shawls completed their ensembles.

The door slammed shut, and Daniel urged me down a hallway. I recognized the faded-red carpet, and I wasn't surprised when we stopped in front of his cabin. He opened the door with a bronze skeleton key and pulled me inside.

Daylight poured through the portholes. Daniel grabbed up his red robe and wrapped me into it before dropping me into a wooden chair near a small tea table. He stood back to glare at me, hands laced behind his back.

"Well?" I asked. "I see you found your robe." I burrowed into it. The *Vigilance* was much colder than the *Century Star*.

"Well indeed," he said. "You are causing me a great deal of trouble. Do you have any notion of how distraught I was to find you gone? I had no notion of what happened to you, whether some mishap had befallen you or whether I might find you firmly ensconced in the dining room *en dishabille*. Or perhaps seated in the captain's office, explaining that I had secreted you away in a cabin for nefarious purposes. At one point in my search for you this morning, I wondered if in fact you *had* been a dream, as you suggested."

"Oh!" I murmured. I dropped my eyes to his well-polished black shoes. "Well, thank you."

"I did not mean *that* kind of dream, madam!"

"You don't really need to be so rude, Dr. Hawthorne." To my chagrin, tears formed in my, eyes and my voice grew husky. I blamed my heightened emotions on the anniversary of Jeff's death.

I heard a sharp intake of breath and a muttered curse, and a clean linen handkerchief appeared in front of my face. I took it without looking up and wiped at my cheeks.

"I'm sorry. I'm not usually this sensitive."

"It is I who should apologize, Mrs. Wollam. There is no need for me to treat you so boorishly. I do not have a vast amount of experience with the sensitivities of women, treating sailors more often as I often do. I was concerned when I could not find you this morning. Thomas said the bed in the cabin was tidy, appearing not to have been slept in. My robe had been left on a chair. Did you sleep on deck? You must have been chilled."

"I don't think so," I said, hanging on to his handkerchief. "I remember laying down on top of the covers of the bottom bunk in the stewards' cabin, and then this morning I woke up in my own cabin."

"On this ship? Do you have a cabin on this ship then?"

"No, on the *Century Star*."

"The *Century Star*? You are on the *Vigilance*, Mrs. Wollam. I thought I made that clear."

"I'm dreaming," I said flatly with a shrug of my shoulders.

"Yes, you said that. But you are not. This ship is not a dream. *I* am not a dream."

I actually thought he *was* kind of dreamy, but I remained silent.

"Do you suffer from memory loss, Mrs. Wollam? Have you had episodes such as this before? That might explain why you are on the ship, although not really how you managed to board without a ticket. You mentioned that you are widowed? Did your husband die recently?"

I shook my head.

"No, not really. He died two years ago this month."

"Ah! This month! I see. Please accept my condolences, Mrs. Wollam." He hesitated for a moment before continuing. "It is quite possible that you are suffering from some form of psychosis stemming from your grief."

"Psychosis? So you think I'm nuts?" I wasn't offended. His theory probably had some merit.

"Please, Mrs. Wollam. I would never use such a vulgar term. It is a possible explanation, however, for your delusions."

"Doc, I'm dreaming, not deluded."

"And I say you are not in a dream, madam."

"How do you know?"

He looked around as if to find proof. Finding none, he returned his attention to me.

"I simply know."

"I think we're going to have to agree to disagree, Dr. Hawthorne. Besides, if this is a dream, it's not going to last long, right? I don't think I've ever had a dream that encompassed a period of years, weeks or even days. Have you?"

He shook his head. "No, I must say that I have not. Do you dream often?"

"No, actually. I haven't dreamed in years, not that I know of. I'm not sure why I am now."

"Perhaps the onset is stimulated by the anniversary of your husband's death."

I nodded. "Maybe."

Daniel gave himself a visible shake.

"No! I will not allow myself to become distracted by such notions. You are *not* dreaming at this moment."

"I fell asleep on my balcony on the *Century Star* just a few moments ago. Last night I laid down on a bunk in the stewards' cabin. Before that, I'd been sleeping in my bed on the *Century Star*. That's three for three, Doc. If it walks like a duck..."

Daniel opened his mouth to speak, but at a knock on the door, he put his finger to his lips—yet again—and moved to the door. He opened it a crack and then let Thomas in.

"Madam! There you are!" the teenager exclaimed.

"Thomas, remember your place," Daniel said, though he put an affectionate hand on the boy's shoulder. "Please be so good as to bring us some tea and sandwiches. Mrs. Wollam will stay in my cabin for the time being. I will sleep in the infirmary office tonight."

"Yes, sir. Right away." Thomas threw another relieved glance at me and left.

"I doubt I'll be here by tonight, but thank you. Your cabin is much larger than Thomas's."

"Yes, I am aware of that." Daniel crossed the room to open the trunk. He spoke over his shoulder while searching for something.

"I have struggled with the notion of asking one of our two lady passengers for a gown but cannot devise a suitable explanation. Even I cannot in all conscience keep you trapped in a cabin for the length of the trip. We will not reach our next port at Tahiti for five more days." He closed the lid of the trunk with a sigh.

"I do not want to bring your presence to the captain's attention. I am not at all certain that he would not lock you up as a stowaway. And that *would* be in steerage, though I am not quite sure where. I have nothing with which to dress you, nothing that would fit, but you and Thomas are of a size. I will ask him to bring some clothing for you to wear. I warn you though, Mrs. Wollam—you will only be able to leave the cabin for fresh air when accompanied by me, and probably late at night or before dawn."

I smiled at Daniel and shrugged but said nothing. Moonlight walks on deck. Sure.

Thomas returned in a moment with a tray, which he set on the table nearest me. Suddenly hungry, I grabbed a sandwich and bit in while Daniel poured tea. He took the seat across from me and looked up at the teen.

"Thomas, lad, this may sound like an unusual request, and I know you will bear with me, but could I borrow a set of your clothes? A blouse, trousers, jacket, stockings and shoes? I will, of course, be happy to reimburse you."

"My clothes, sir?" Thomas stammered.

"Aye, your clothes, if you please. Clean, washed and pressed."

"Right away, sir." Thomas left the room.

"Poor kid," I said. "But you're right though. He's about five foot two, and so am I. How old is he?"

"Thomas is seventeen, small for his age. His parents could no longer care for their large brood of children, so they gave him over to the captain. I took him on as my cabin steward when I saw the other lads bullying him because of his small size. He assists me in the infirmary as well."

I noticed that Daniel seemed to be making more eye contact with me than before, and I wondered if his reserve was melting.

"Are you shy?" I asked abruptly.

Daniel's cheeks bronzed.

"I beg your pardon?"

"Are you shy? Reserved? Were you shy as a child?"

"I am most certainly not shy, madam. But yes, I was shy as a child. I was a sickly child, often ill with difficulty breathing. We now know that I had asthma from the coal dust in New York City. I saw the doctor so often that I wanted to be like him. And so I became a physician. I think your alternate description of reserved is probably apt."

I smiled at him.

"How is your asthma now?"

"Vanished, resolved. The warm humid air of the South Pacific helps a great deal. My parents passed away, and I have no other family, so I do not return to New York. I keep rooms in San Francisco, and though coal dust is prevalent in the city, I am not there enough to be troubled by the air."

"So you like the South Pacific?"

"Immensely," he said with a nod. "I hope to buy a house there one day and set up practice there, perhaps in a few years. Perhaps in 1850. That is a good round number."

My teacup rattled as I dropped it onto the saucer.

"Are you saying it's 1847?"

"Well, of course it is, Mrs. Wollam."

"1847," I breathed. Well, of course! I thought the women had been dressed in Victorian-era clothing. The *Vigilance* lacked the amenities of a modern ship. I had seen no electricity, no plumbing.

"Odd that I'm dreaming about 1847. What's significant about that year? Anything?" I looked to Daniel for an answer, but he had none. He didn't believe me anyway.

"Then you continue to believe that this is a dream, madam?"

I nodded.

"Oh, yes."

"And you do not remember stowing away aboard the ship?"

"Not even in my dream."

Daniel shook his head and swallowed some of his tea, ignoring the food.

"I am at a loss, madam. I cannot even imagine what I will do with you over the next week until we reach Tahiti. I struggle to imagine how we shall proceed even over the next day."

I blinked as I looked at Daniel. An inordinate sense of fatigue overwhelmed me at that moment, draining me of energy. The cabin seemed warm, too warm. I shrugged the robe off my shoulders and set my teacup and saucer down on the table.

"I feel so sleepy," I mumbled. "It just hit me. I haven't been sleeping well, as you can imagine. I am so tired."

Despite my best efforts, my eyelids drooped.

I heard Daniel's voice as if from far away.

"Mrs. Wollam? Mrs. Wollam?"

CHAPTER THREE

I opened my eyes to the sight of white-capped blue seas drifting by. The sun peeped through a vast expanse of clouds. Beads of humid moisture covered the arms of my deck chair and the balcony bannister. Sweat poured down my forehead and the sides of my face.

I pushed myself out of my chair and staggered into my cabin, my sea leg giving out beneath me. Dropping onto my bed, I allowed the air conditioning to waft over me and cool down my overheated body.

"It is a dream," I said mournfully. "I'm just dreaming."

My first instinct was to run out into the hallway, to look for the faded-red carpet, to find Daniel's cabin, to find Daniel. But Daniel wasn't real. He was just a dream.

And a time traveling dream at that. Daniel said the year was 1847. I could think of no particular reason why I would dream about 1847, or 1850 or any other year, in fact. If I were going to travel back in time in a dream, wouldn't I have traveled back a few years and dragged Jeff in to see a brain surgeon to fix his aneurysm?

Was it possible that I could travel back two years in my dream, to talk to Jeff one more time? I pressed my eyes shut and muttered the year. Gritting my teeth, I willed myself to dream about Jeff, about a time before he passed away.

But exhausted as I was, sleep now eluded me. The harder I tried to sleep, the busier my mind grew. Memories of Jeff intermingled with guilty thoughts of Daniel made my pulse pound. Sleep seemed an impossibility.

I rose with a sigh, dressed in my swimsuit and cover-up and made my way to the nearest pool. After showering poolside, I stepped down into the pool and floated around, letting the swaying of the ship swish me back and forth across the surface of the water.

Cloudy skies didn't deter from the abundant sunshine. Unlike Seattle's commonly thick gray weather, clouds over the South Pacific Ocean gently filtered sunlight, allowing warm rays to caress my face.

I sloshed about in the pool, wondering about Daniel. Did he swim? Had he ever been married? Was he married in my dream? He'd said he wanted to buy a house in the South Pacific. Where? Tahiti?

I clung to the side of the pool and wondered if I would see him again in my dreams. If he was married, that would be pointless. Surely I could control whether or not Daniel was married, couldn't I? I scrunched my face, certain in the knowledge that I had very little control of my dreams at the moment.

I climbed out of the pool, toweled off and returned to my room for a shower. As I dressed in a yellow flowered skirt and matching tank top, I thought about the elaborate dresses the ladies on the *Vigilance* had worn, and I wondered if I could do justice to the long flowing lines of their gowns in a painting. I had never painted fashion before, preferring landscapes, but something about the memory of the ladies promenading on the deck compelled me to grab the notepad I never traveled without and sketch the scene before I forgot it.

I finished the sketch within half an hour and stared at the figures, wondering if I'd remembered them correctly. I colored in the sketch to show one woman's dress of royal-blue silk adorned with black ribbons. A matching bonnet of blue satin perched on her silver hair. Ringlets framed her cheeks. I thought I recalled the other woman's dress as gray satin and cream lace, with a dark hat as well, perhaps a dark charcoal.

I set the sketch aside and stared at my blank pad. As if under its own power, my pencil outlined the oval of a man's face. The image of Daniel's wavy dark hair and thick eyebrows emerged. I colored his long almond eyes nut brown. Accenting the cleft in his chin, I gave him the five-o'clock shadow I had seen on him the night before.

I stared at the sketch, wondering how I could compel the dream again. I wanted to see Daniel one more time. I wanted to see Jeff too, but no amount of tears or longing had brought Jeff back over the past two years.

In a restless motion, I tossed my pad aside and left the room, heading down to the shops to while away some time before dinner.

I picked up a few souvenir T-shirts for friends and stopped to look at clothing off the rack. Having no intention of dressing up or mingling with other happy couples, I hadn't brought anything to wear on the formal dinner nights on the ship. T-shirts, shorts and yoga pants had been simple enough to pack.

I fingered an ankle-length formfitting island-flowered dress that seemed to stretch all four ways. Resembling a wide-skirted Victorian dress not at all, I nevertheless bought it on a whim, with the vague idea of wearing it to bed. Just in case I dreamed that night. Hoping that I dreamed that night.

I returned my purchases to my room and checked the time. Six o'clock. The afternoon had seemed interminable, and it appeared that the evening would drag just as much. I ran up to the buffet for a quick dinner and returned to my room by seven.

The hour was still too early for bed, but I didn't care. I slipped into the sleeveless dress that I'd bought, pulled my hair up into a semblance of a chignon and plopped down onto my bed.

Catching sight of my bare feet, I drew in a sharp breath. Shoes! I needed shoes. I ran to my closet and slipped into one of two pairs of flip-flops that I'd brought, the only style of shoes other than sneakers that I had packed. As an afterthought, I brushed my teeth, applied a bit of eye makeup and lipstick and returned to my bed. Turning out the lights, I stared into the darkness and began to repeat a silent mantra as if to hypnotize myself.

Sleep. Sleep. Sleep. Please sleep.

I had failed to force myself to sleep earlier that afternoon. Could I make it work this time? Would I see Jeff? Daniel? Would I fail?

Sleep. Sleep. Sleep.

I opened my eyes to the sight of Daniel's back as he sat at his desk. Hatless but otherwise fully dressed in his dark uniform jacket, he appeared to be writing something.

"Daniel?"

Daniel whirled around and jumped up from his chair.

"Margaret? Mrs. Wollam? Where did you come from? Where did you go? How is this possible?"

I swung my feet off the bed and stood. The look in Daniel's eyes as he studied me from head to foot brought a flush to my cheeks.

"I'm dreaming again, aren't I?" I asked.

Daniel moved toward me, taking my hands in his.

"No, you are not dreaming, but I begin to think that perhaps I am. Your hands are cold."

"Yours are warm," I murmured. I dropped my eyes from the intensity of his gaze.

"I think I must not let you go lest you disappear again," he murmured.

"I don't know if I can stop this. I'm dreaming. I went to sleep with the express intention of coming back again."

"Why?" He chuckled and shook his head, the first time I heard him laugh. "No, not why did you sleep, but why did you come back?"

I looked down at our joined hands again but said nothing. I bit my lip with frustration at my inhibition even within the dream. I should have felt free to say anything I wanted, to tell Daniel that I had missed him that afternoon.

"You do not answer. Come. Sit." He led me back to the chair where I had sat before, and he took his seat across from me. The teacups and sandwiches remained on the table between us.

"I was just journaling." Daniel pointed to an open book on the desk. "About you. When you vanished before my eyes, I realized that you did not in fact stow away. You were not spirited aboard nor kidnapped. Some supernatural force is at work here, and I do not understand it."

"Probably not," I mumbled. I stared at his large hands, wishing they still held mine in their clasp.

"Then help me understand." He leaned toward me, placing his elbows on his knees.

"I mean, I don't think anything supernatural is going on. It's just a dream."

"And do you often sleep in such festive gowns?"

I looked up to see his eyes running over me. My cheeks flamed.

"No." I took a chance. "I bought it just in case I dreamed again." I omitted "about you." "It's not exactly Victorian, but it's all I could find in the shop aboard ship that went down to my ankles."

"Victorian?"

"The Victorian era? You said it's 1847, right? I think that's the Victorian era, isn't it?"

"Yes, I believe it is called such, though I am American. Are you suggesting that you were not aware of the year, Mrs. Wollam? How can that possibly be?" He leaned forward as if to study my face more thoroughly. "You are nothing if not mysterious, madam. You say you are dreaming, which you are not. But given that you believe you might be, what year do you believe it is?"

"2018, the twenty-first century."

Daniel sucked in a sharp breath and reared his head back. He stared at me, his jaw open.

"What?"

"The twenty-first century," I murmured, picking at a nonexistent spot on my dress, near my knee. "In my dream."

He opened his mouth and then closed it again, as if he couldn't find words. I peeked up at him from under my lashes.

"Are you shocked?"

Daniel nodded slowly, tilting his head and studying me. My cheeks flamed. Finally, he spoke.

"Mrs. Wollam, I-I do not know what to say. The twenty-first century? How is that possible?"

I shrugged. "I'm not sure."

"But why? Why now? Why do you travel to this time?"

"Travel? Do you mean...like time travel? Oh, I don't think that's happening. That's not possible."

"And dreaming is?"

"Well..." I had no answer.

I heard the sound of bells in the hallway, and Daniel glanced at the door.

"It is time for dinner. I am expected to dine with the captain and guests tonight." He looked at me, and I tried not to show my disappointment. I didn't know when I would awaken and vanish again.

"Yet I dare not leave you here alone."

I tried not to read too much into his statement, by my foolish heart heard what it wanted to hear. I had rapidly become infatuated with the stranger in my dream, and I worried about my loss of control. Had I been so very lonely since my husband's death that I'd fallen for an imaginary character in a dream?

"I will ask Thomas to pass along my compliments to the captain and make my excuses. I shall say that I am ill. Are you hungry? Would you care for some dinner here in the cabin?"

"I just ate actually, but I'm sure you're hungry."

"I will have Thomas bring something for both of us in case you change your mind. Perhaps you can stay awhile this time." Daniel stood up to head for the door.

"I hope so."

At my words, he turned and smiled, the expression lightening his face. My heart flopped in my chest. How odd that the flash of teeth could make his handsome face that much more charming.

"Good! Do not leave! I will only be a moment." Daniel spun around and left the room. I gripped the edge of the table, trying to hang on to the present, trying desperately not to slip away. I didn't feel sleepy, but I had drifted off before.

Thankfully, Daniel returned in a few minutes. Rushing into the room, he took one look at me and came to a stop.

"There you are!"

"Here I am," I said with a grin.

"Thomas will bring dinner soon. By the way, Thomas did bring a set of his clothing. I laid them by. Perhaps you can wear them in the morning, provided that you are still here."

Daniel indicated a pile of folded clothing lying on top of the trunk.

"In the meantime, tell me about your life in the twenty-first century. For whether you are dreaming or traveling through time, I know nothing about the twenty-first century."

He sat down and gave me his full attention. Flustered, I found myself stammering.

"Well, I don't really know how to describe it really. What do you want to know?"

"Tell me about medicine. Is there finally a cure for typhus? I have heard shiploads of Irish immigrants fleeing famine have arrived in Canada with typhus."

I shook my head. "I don't know. I think so. Probably with antibiotics." I told him what little I knew about antibiotics. I told him about planes and automobiles, computers and the Internet, space and deep-sea exploration. And I asked Daniel questions about his time—what sort of a ship we were on, what diseases were rampant in his time, how women fared both physically and legally.

"Have you any theories as to why you appear in 1847 versus any other time? We can infer that you appear on this ship because it appears to be following a similar course as your *Century Star*, no? You did say you were on your way to Tahiti?"

"Yes, Tahiti. And no, I don't know why I dream about 1847."

"Do you have a particular interest in this era?"

"I don't think so. I didn't anyway. I do now."

His normally somber expression lightened a bit again.

"How fortunate for us," he murmured.

A knock on the door brought Thomas, whose blue eyes widened at the sight of me. He too studied my dress, and I crossed my arms self-consciously. He eyed the pile of clothing on the trunk but said nothing as he set a tray of food, wine and glasses on the table.

"Thank you, Thomas. Did the captain take the news in stride?"

"Aye, Doctor. Mr. Sedgewick had been pining for a seat at the table, and the captain was able to accommodate him."

"All is well, then. Thank you again. I will pour the wine."

Thomas backed out, and I eyed the wine.

"Oh, I don't think that's a good idea for me. Any mind-altering product is probably going to wake me up."

"Or send you back through time."

"You don't give up, do you?"

"Not if I think I am right."

I actually joined Daniel in eating while he told me more of his childhood in New York. His father had been a doctor. From his description of his mother's social activities and a few favorite servants—his nanny and the housekeeper—I deduced that Daniel came from money.

"And you said that your parents had passed away?"

"Yes, they died in a carriage accident quite unexpectedly several years ago. Mrs. Griggs, the housekeeper, takes care of the house in my absence. Which, as I mentioned, is often."

"Yes, between sailing and your place in San Francisco, I'm surprised you haven't sold the house in New York."

"I cannot. It has been in the family for generations. I would not dare."

"Well, maybe you can leave it for your children."

"I do not believe that I will have children," he said quietly.

"Oh, really? Why?"

His cheeks bronzed once again.

"One would have to be married to have children. Given my career at sea, I do not meet many eligible women."

I wondered about Polynesian women but said nothing.

"But you do have female passengers, don't you?" I grinned. Both ladies I had seen appeared to be quite a bit older than Daniel.

"Yes, we do, though only the two ladies on this voyage. Or three." Again, that handsome smile. "Still, there is little occasion for me to form an attachment to a passenger. It is generally frowned upon to fraternize other than in one's capacity as a ship's officer."

"Will you always be a ship's doctor? You don't even have to work, do you?"

"What do you mean?" he asked, helping himself to a glass of wine.

"Well, you mention a family home in New York, a housekeeper, rooms in San Francisco. I'm assuming you are comfortable."

"Ah! Are you asking if I am wealthy?"

"Only in that you don't have to spend the rest of your life at sea."

"No, I do not need to sail the world to support myself. You are right. But I enjoy my profession, and I enjoy life at sea. For a while longer, at any rate."

"So, no children."

"No, probably not. And you, Mrs. Wollam? I never asked. Do you have children?" He straightened. "Goodness! Do you? They must be very young if you do. Who takes care of them while you sail?"

"No, no children. My husband and I did not have children before he died."

"May I ask how your husband died? If you do not wish to answer, I understand."

"No, that's all right. He had a brain aneurysm at twenty-eight."

"My condolences," he murmured.

"Thank you. Jeff had his own law practice, specializing in estate planning, and you can imagine, he planned his own estate well, leaving me wanting for nothing. Except a husband. And children."

Tears formed in my eyes. I held my breath and blinked them away.

"I am so sorry."

"Thank you."

"You are still young. I trust you will marry again."

"Maybe." I didn't want to talk about my future anymore. I only wanted to live in the present with the dreamy doctor.

"Do you think we could take a walk on deck yet?"

Daniel set his wineglass down and looked out one of the portholes. Night had fallen.

"Yes, I think we could chance it for a moment. Most guests will still be dining. I will give you Thomas's jacket, as the night breezes will be cool."

"And my dress is still kind of revealing? For 1847?"

"Perhaps," he said. The corners of his lips twitched, and my heart rolled over.

He picked up Thomas's dark jacket and settled it over my shoulders. I followed him to the door, where he looked out before signaling forward. With a hand at the small of my back, he guided me down the hallway until we reached the wooden door that opened onto the deck. He pushed the door open, and we emerged onto a breezy dark night.

Daniel tucked my hand under his arm as we walked. In the absence of lighting, the moon, thankfully full, shed some light on the deck. The night wind blew strong, loosening my chignon. I grabbed at my hair to hold it in place.

"Let it go," Daniel said. "The winds are strong at night, and you have no hope of keeping your coiffure in place. Your hair looks lovely blowing in the breeze."

Daniel stopped and turned to me. He reached up as if to push a reddish-brown lock from my face. I closed my eyes.

CHAPTER FOUR

Just then, I heard voices. Apparently so did Daniel, because he pulled me under a dark stairwell.

The ladies I had seen before strolled by, accompanied by an elderly gentleman carrying a cane in one hand and holding on to his top hat with the other hand. The ladies, now dressed in bright silks of silver and green, eschewed bonnets in favor of girlish beribboned bows laced through their coifs. Silver ringlets blew in the wind.

"I think we should have heeded your advice not to attempt a stroll tonight, Mr. Asher. I concede that it is far too windy out here. Will you kindly take us back inside?" the woman in green said.

"Yes, of course, Mrs. Darymple. I am sorry to have been right about the wind, but there you are."

I rolled my eyes at Daniel.

The threesome reentered the interior ship by a nearby doorway.

"Ah, yes. Mr. Asher," Daniel murmured. "He has sailed with us before. I have heard him lament that he cannot find a wife, and he wonders why."

I laughed out loud.

Daniel pulled me out from underneath the stairwell.

"I think we may feel confident that the other passengers will find the deck too windy, and so we may proceed with our walk if you wish."

"I do wish." I stuck my hand under Daniel's arm again, and we promenaded in near darkness, buffeted off balance a few times, which made me laugh. Even Daniel chuckled, a sound that warmed my heart.

"Before you go again, how can we control this coming and going of yours?"

"I don't know," I said, shaking my head. "I really don't know. I wish I did."

"It is no good asking you not to sleep, if that is how you believe you are traveling back and forth."

"I'm afraid that won't work. I'll just fall asleep when I'm exhausted."

"Yes, I noticed," he said in a dry voice. "And then you vanished." Daniel pressed my hand tightly against his side, and my knees weakened at the almost possessive gesture. I relished the intimacy of the moment. My pulse pounded in my throat, my heart.

As if Daniel could feel my chaotic emotions, he looked down at me. I put a nervous hand to my hair to push it back.

"Have you had enough fresh air?" he asked.

"Yes," I said. "We can go back inside."

We entered his cabin, and he let me go with seeming reluctance. I retook my seat and watched as he poured himself another glass of wine. I would have loved a glass of the ruby liquid but dared not. I noted the disappearance of the tray of food and surmised that Thomas must have cleared it away.

Daniel and I talked throughout the night. I thought I would struggle with drowsiness, but I remained alert. Was it possible that I slept soundly in my own time, thereby allowing me to stay with Daniel?

It seemed as if both of us were starved for conversation. He spoke of his life on the sea as a merchant ship's doctor, and I told him about my painting. We shared the common bond of lonely childhoods with inattentive parents. His parents had traveled a great deal but left him home with the housekeeper. My parents had socialized excessively, both ultimately drinking and smoking themselves into early graves by the time I was twenty-two.

The wind grew stronger overnight, and the ship bounced around in the ocean. Rain began to pelt the portholes.

"It seems we have run into a storm," Daniel said, rising to look out of one of the windows. "The sea has grown rough. Swells are high." He pulled a pocket watch from a pocket in his jacket.

"It is nearly dawn. I will fetch us some fresh hot tea and toast. Stay in the cabin. The deck will no doubt be awash with waves, and it would not be safe for you outside."

Daniel left, and I listened to the creaking of the ship. I'd only taken cruises twice before with Jeff, and I didn't consider myself a confident sailor. I had to admit that I was worried. The ship groaned beneath me, and furniture began to slide around in Daniel's cabin. A loud thud and shudder shook the ship.

I looked up at the porthole. Rain lashed against the window, rattling it. The ship suddenly rolled from side to side.

Panicked, I jumped up and made my way to the cabin door by holding on to whatever furniture didn't move. I needed Daniel's reassuring presence.

I pulled open the door and looked out into the hallway. Darkness prevailed, but as people began to emerge from their cabins in various states of undress, holding candles and lanterns aloft, I saw that the ship listed slightly to the starboard side. Mrs. Darymple and her companion emerged into the hallway. In disarray as if they'd dressed hurriedly, the older women clutched at each other as they struggled for balance.

Thomas nimbly ran down the hallway toward me.

"Mrs. Wollam, the doctor says you are to come to the infirmary. Several crew members have been injured in an explosion. He cannot leave, but he thinks you would be safer with him than in the cabin alone."

I followed Thomas down the hall. So panicked were the passengers that no one even seemed to notice me. Mr. Asher emerged from his cabin, holding up a lantern.

"Young man! Young man, what is going on?"

At that moment, several crew members hurried into the hallway and ordered the passengers to collect in the dining room.

Thomas paused and bit his lip, as if he was thinking.

"Thomas! What's happening?" I almost shouted above another loud groan of the ship.

"I think the ship is in danger of sinking, Mrs. Wollam. Come! We have to find the doctor. He will know what to do. It's just down one deck."

Shouts and shrieks from frightened passengers followed me as I hurried after Thomas. I definitely didn't want to descend any farther into the ship, but I wanted to find Daniel.

We clattered down the stairs and emerged onto the deck that housed Thomas's cabin. Instead of turning right toward his room, we turned left. Thomas led me to an open doorway, where we found Daniel, his jacket thrown aside, shirtsleeves rolled up, tending to two men who looked severely burnt. I stopped short in shock. I had never seen anything so awful in my life as charred human skin. The smell overwhelmed me.

"Thomas, tend to the men," Daniel said. He hurried toward me, pulled me into his arms and whispered into my ear.

"If you have the ability to travel back to your time, go now!" he said. "The ship is sinking. I do not think we are near land. Go, Maggie. Go!"

I clung to Daniel when he tried to pull away from me.

"I can't just make it happen! Don't leave me, Daniel."

"Please go, Maggie. Do what you must to save yourself."

Daniel kissed my hand and turned away. He returned to one of the men's sides. I saw Thomas shake his head, and Daniel moved onto the second man. His shoulders sagged, and he turned back to me, his face stricken. I knew that the men were dead.

Another groan of the ship terrified me and galvanized Daniel into action. He grabbed Thomas by the back of his jacket and pulled him toward the door, grabbing me up on the way.

"Off we go!" He propelled us out the doorway and down the hall. Crew members ran past us, oblivious to us, to me. Daniel pushed Thomas up the stairs and half carried me up in a whirl.

We reached the heavy wooden door leading to the deck, but it stuck. Together, we three pushed against the door and managed to open it a crack. Rain forced its way in, painfully pelting our faces. Wind screamed through the partially opened door.

"Keep pushing!" Daniel shouted above the noise.

A heavy weight landed on my back, and I looked over my shoulder to see two crew members launching themselves against the door to help open it. Although I found myself smothered in the mix of bodies, I welcomed the help of the young men, whose aprons suggested they either cooked or served food.

"Thank you, boys!" Daniel shouted as the door opened fully. An assault of horrific weather pounded us as we emerged onto what must have been the port side of the deck. The ship listed such that we couldn't plant both feet squarely on the deck. Daniel gave Thomas an almost vertical boost to reach the railing, and then he pushed me above him. The crewmen scrambled over us, and while one hung on to Thomas, the other, a short burly blond, grabbed me with both hands, pulling me up.

I grabbed the railing, wrapped my arms around it and held on, shouting for Daniel. The blond who had grabbed me held out a hand, and Daniel grasped it to pull himself up beside me.

"Are you all right?" he shouted. "Thomas, boys?"

I nodded and turned to look at Thomas, clinging to the rail on my left.

His teeth chattered, but he nodded. The tall, lanky dark-haired crewman who had helped Thomas kept hold of him around the waist.

"We must get to a boat!" Daniel shouted to the men.

Through thick sheets of rain and a terrifying roaring of the sea as it attempted to suck the ship down, I heard nearby shouts and screams. I looked down to see another crew member trying to help Mrs. Darymple and her companion reach the railing.

"Stay put, Thomas," Daniel shouted.

I screamed as he let go and slid down the deck to help the group.

"Daniel!"

The crewmen who had helped us let go as well and scrambled down to aid the older women.

I sobbed in terror as the ship shuddered, and I reached out to wrap an arm around Thomas's frame. I hadn't realized how thin he was, and my maternal instinct kicked in as I felt him shaking.

"Everything's going to be all right, Thomas. Everything's going to be all right."

"Yes, miss," he chattered.

All four men rather heroically pushed, pulled and prodded the ladies up to the railing. The women, hampered by the weight of their thick rain-soaked skirts, could do little to help. I only hoped those beautiful dresses didn't drown them. I hoped we all didn't drown. If I had ever been going to awaken, that moment would have been ideal. But I prayed I wouldn't.

Please don't wake up, I prayed silently. *Please don't wake up. I can't bear to leave Daniel. Not like this.*

"Look, Doctor!" the tall dark-haired crewman called out. "One of the boats!" He pointed over the edge of the railing toward a wooden skiff heaving in the roiling water four decks below. Empty, it seemed to wait for us. But we would have to jump for it. I doubted any of us could survive landing in the boat, not without breaking a few bones, and I worried that the ladies could not survive a jump straight down into the water.

"The ladies can't make that!" I said, leaning in toward Daniel's ear.

He turned to me.

"They have to! Can you swim?" he asked, shouting over the wind and rain.

I nodded, unsure if my previous snorkeling experience was enough training for the tempestuous waters below but unwilling to add to Daniel's burden. He appeared to have taken the welfare of our little group upon his shoulders.

"Good! Stay by me, and watch over Thomas if you can. He's a good swimmer." He turned and shouted to the taller crewman. "I will take Mrs. Darymple. Frederick, take Mrs. Simpson." He indicated the companion. "We have to jump!"

"No need. I may be old, but I am a strong swimmer," Mrs. Darymple snapped in a querulous but determined voice. "Take care of Agatha!"

Daniel nodded toward Fredrick, who took hold of the sobbing gray-haired Mrs. Simpson.

Daniel crawled over my body and positioned himself between Thomas and me.

"Follow me!" he shouted over his shoulders toward the group.

Before I was fully aware of what was happening, Daniel pulled Thomas and I over the edge of the railing, and without pause he jumped, taking us with him.

I screamed, then drew in a sharp breath as the churning ocean rose up to smash against my legs. Plummeting down into the cold depths, I kicked hard toward the surface. I had long ago lost my flip-flops. I didn't quite realize when. Salt water burned my eyes, and I couldn't orient myself. I'd lost Daniel and Thomas on entry into the water. Panicked, I kicked once again, hoping I was heading in the right direction.

An arm slid around my waist, and I looked up to see Daniel close to my face, his hair billowing in the water. Thomas swam close to him, one hand on Daniel's back.

Daniel kicked hard and pulled us upward, and we emerged to gasp air. Waves, wind and rain battered me, and Daniel grabbed my hand as we kicked for the boat. Thomas stayed close.

Ahead, I could see the men crawling into the boat and pulling the two women with them. Thomas swam ahead toward the boat, and one of the men leaned over, grabbed his outstretched arms and hauled him in.

"Doctor!" Thomas turned and called out. "This way!"

Daniel and I reached the side of the wildly rocking skiff.

"Wait for a wave," Daniel shouted. He grabbed me around the waist and on the crest of a wave, threw me up over the lip of the hull. The men grabbed me and pulled me in, dropping me on the floorboards.

I jumped up to ensure that Daniel followed closely behind me.

But he didn't. A cresting wave carried him away from the boat, and I screamed for him.

"Daniel! Daniel!" I rose, prepared to jump in after him, but I heard his voice.

"No, Maggie! Stay!"

He fought his way out of the wave and turned back to us, kicking wildly, his arms cleaving through the rough waters.

I sobbed as he neared the boat.

"Daniel!" I shouted raggedly.

Daniel raised a hand, and the blond grabbed it. I leaned over, doing nothing more than getting in the way, as the three crew members and Thomas reached for Daniel to haul him into the boat. Daniel fell onto the floorboards in an exhausted mess, and I grabbed one of his cold hands.

"Thank you! Thank you!" I said to the men, now grabbing two sets of oars in the boat. Mrs. Darymple and Mrs. Simpson huddled together on the aft benches.

"Go, sit with the women, Maggie," Daniel ordered. He pulled my hand to his lips before giving me a gentle shove. I crawled my way aft and hunkered down at their feet, no room left on the benches.

"Come, girl. Sit here," Mrs. Darymple ordered. She moved over, but I shook my head.

"No, I'm fine down here. I feel safer!"

"Row away from the ship before she sucks us under," Daniel yelled. "Look for survivors!" He shrugged out of his sodden jacket, took hold of one of the oars and pulled hard, helping turn the bow of the lifeboat away from the sinking ship.

I rose up to my knees and looked over the edge of the hull. A horrific sight, the three-masted ship listed to the right and appeared to be sinking in a swell of waves. I couldn't watch, and I turned away to see the muscles in Daniel's back strain against his wet shirt as he pulled at the oars, taking us safely away from the undertow of the doomed ship.

CHAPTER FIVE

A hand touched my face, and I awakened with a start. Daniel leaned over me, shielding me from the sun.

"I'm still here!" I murmured.

He put a finger to his lips and threw a warning glance toward the two sleeping women sprawled in an awkward position over the bench in the rear of the boat.

"Yes, you are," he whispered. "More is the pity."

"I'm fine." In those words and the glance of affection that I gave Daniel, I meant more than I said. He blinked and tilted his head with an expression of curiosity, like a puppy trying to understand human speech. His black hair, normally well groomed, curled over his forehead. He had unbuttoned his collar, his neckcloth having disappeared, and rolled up his shirtsleeves. His clothing was now dry, and I realized I must have fallen asleep sometime after we watched the ship sink beneath the water.

"Where are we?" I asked, rubbing my eyes. I looked over the lip of the skiff at a vast ocean of blue broken only by small whitecaps. The sea had calmed, and the boat bobbed gently, thankfully. A mild breeze blew through my hair, my chignon long gone. I reached to push it back off my face but encountered Daniel's hand already there, smoothing it back from my forehead. I grasped his hand.

"I'm so glad you're alive," I whispered.

"And to my shame, I am so glad that you are here," he muttered. He brought my hand to his mouth and released it quickly, turning away hastily to scan the horizon. With a melting heart, I watched a muscle tick in his jaw.

"I do not know where we are," Daniel continued after a moment. "I am a doctor, not a navigator, unfortunately. The other men, Frederick and James, worked in the kitchen, and Samuel is a steward." Daniel looked over his shoulder toward the men rowing the boat. "But no matter where we are, I should return to rowing. We have seen a few birds, so we hope that we are near land. But in which direction, I cannot say."

Daniel touched the tip of my already sunburned nose and returned to his oar. I turned and looked at the women, worried about their exposure to sun under the largely cloudless sky. I saw Thomas huddled, fast asleep, in a shaded crevice at the front of the boat.

I rose and held on to the edge of the skiff as I studied the ladies. Devoid of hats, their reddened faces showed the effects of the sun, and I thought they would be best served if they slipped down to the shade under the bench seats. I shook Mrs. Darymple gently.

She came awake with a start, her hands batting at me before she realized who I was.

"What is it, girl? What is happening?"

"Nothing, Mrs. Darymple!" I straightened. Mrs. Simpson awakened as well and sat up straight, looking out over the ocean with a bewildered expression.

"You are getting too much sun," I said "I think you and Mrs. Simpson should lay down on the bottom of the boat under the bench. There's a little bit of shade there."

"On the floorboards?" Mrs. Simpson asked in a confused voice.

"Yes, Agatha, the floorboards. The girl is quite right. We must shelter ourselves. I suspect we are lost, and we must conserve strength. There is no telling when we will find land with food or drink."

To my surprise, Mrs. Darymple slipped off the bench and pulled Mrs. Simpson with her. Mrs. Darymple crawled as far under the bench as she could, reaching out to settle her now-dry skirts about her legs.

"Come, Agatha."

Mrs. Simpson followed suit, but I worried about her. She seemed disoriented, and I hoped that was just temporary and not some more permanent damage from the trauma of jumping four decks into the water. We had encountered no other survivors as we rowed away from the doomed ship. The storm had eased within half an hour, and the moon had come out long enough to allow us to see the tallest mast of the ship go under, leaving us in no doubt as to its fate.

I returned to my position on the floor and watched the men row, wondering if I could do anything to help. I doubted that Daniel would let me row, nor did I think I could handle the heavy wooden oars.

Several small white-capped gray birds flew overhead and hovered for a moment. I caught my breath and watched them as they studied us. Which way were they headed? Where in the South Pacific were we?

"Daniel!" I called out and pointed to the birds. His haggard face brightened with a grin.

"Terns," he said.

I rose and worked my way over to him, stepping carefully in my bare feet and hanging on to the edge of the bobbing boat.

"Does that mean we're near land?"

Daniel nodded. "Yes, I think so. I am certain of it. The birds cannot be too far from land."

"So do we follow them?"

"Yes, if we can," he said. "I hope they are not heading out to sea to fish though, but we must take our chances." He called out. "Follow the birds, boys!"

"Can I help row?"

"No," Daniel said. "This work is not for women."

"Or doctors," I said.

He gave me a sideways glance, sweat beading his forehead. I hated to see him sweat. It meant he was losing precious fluids, and as Mrs. Darymple had said, we had no idea when we would next find food or fresh water.

"If you would feel better rowing, then you may sit next to me and help pull the oar."

I smiled and joined him on the bench, placing both hands on the oar and pulling in unison with Daniel.

"You are strong for a little thing," he said. "Do you still think you are in a dream?" he asked, lowering his voice and leaning near my ear.

I shook my head. "I don't know, Daniel. I slept, and I'm still here. If I were sleeping in my own time, wouldn't I have awakened by now? It's been how many hours? Twelve?"

"Since you came back? Yes, I think that might be right." He looked up at the sun. "I think it must be about eight o'clock now. The sun rose a few hours ago."

The terns, having investigated us and found nothing to eat, moved on.

"There they go," I said, watching them fly away.

"Yes, that is the direction the other birds have gone. I feel certain there must be land ahead."

Not truly instrumental in helping Daniel row, I leaned over the edge of the boat to see into the distance. A blue-gray haze hovered low on the horizon in front of us.

"I don't know. Could that be land? That haze?"

"Possibly," he said. "Dead ahead, boys! Toward that haze on the horizon."

He seemed energized, and I returned to helping him row. Fairly fit and robust, Daniel hardly needed my help, but I enjoyed being close to him...as long as I could stay.

Several hours later, I worried for him, for all of us. Daniel's lips were dry, and he had ceased to sweat. I noted that Frederick, James and Samuel appeared to struggle as they pulled on the oars. Thomas, having awakened, did his best to rotate among the three men to help row, but given his size, he didn't do much better than I did. Thankfully, the ladies continued to sleep, thereby conserving energy.

"Daniel, that *is* land! I'm sure of it!" I cried out.

"Yes, I believe that you are correct."

I gazed at the dark mass materializing in the distance, and I hoped and prayed it was Hawaii or Tahiti or some other well-populated island, even in the mid-nineteenth century. The island, though, didn't look very large from our vantage point. We were north of the island, as the morning sun was to our left in the east.

The island seemed to grow in size as we approached, but I saw no signs of civilization. No other boats, no smoke, no signs of life. Jagged peaks materialized out of the haze, thrusting toward the sky. I desperately hoped the island boasted a beach where we could easily land the boat. It would be too awful to find an island in the vast ocean where we couldn't land, where we couldn't take shelter.

As the men rowed hard, the swells picked up, as if the sea rushed toward the island. The boat rose and fell accordingly, and I gave up pretending to help Daniel. I hung on to the edge of the skiff and looked over my shoulder to see the women safely ensconced under the bench in the stern.

Turning my attention forward, I saw white surf exploding in the near distance.

"That's a reef, Daniel!" I warned. I had traveled enough that I recognized the breaking waves so far from shore signaled a coral reef and danger to the hull of the boat.

"I know. I know," he muttered. "Hold up, boys!" he shouted. "Reverse the oars. We are approaching a reef." He jumped up, shading his eyes. I clung to his oar, trying to push against it, but couldn't budge the heavy thing on my own.

"Do you see a cut in the reef?" he shouted to the other men. "Any way in?"

A sudden swell knocked Daniel off his feet, but he scrambled up to grab the oar that I clung to.

"I cannot see anything, sir," Frederick shouted. "But we cannot hold the boat back. The surf's got hold of her."

And indeed, the surf pushed us inexorably toward the reef. Beyond the exploding white froth, teal-green water led to the black sands of tranquil-appearing palm-treed beaches, but getting there would be a problem.

"What is happening?" Mrs. Darymple called out. I whirled around to see her on the verge of rising. Mrs. Simpson had awakened as well.

"Stay down, Mrs. Darymple, lest you fall out!" Daniel shouted. "Brace yourselves, ladies. We are in for a rocky ride!"

"We cannot stop the forward motion, Doctor! We are going in!" James yelled.

"Then we must push through. Row for your lives, men. Row!" Daniel shouted, pushing his oar. "Hold tight, everyone!"

I pushed as hard as I could, hoping we could somehow skim above the reef and drop down into the lagoon beyond.

The surf roared, and the bow of the boat rose to crest one of the waves. As we dropped, I heard a horrendous cracking noise, and I knew we had hit the reef. I looked over my shoulder to see a large fracture in the starboard side of the hull. Water flooded the boat in seconds, and I screamed as a second jolt broke the boat apart.

Swept out of the boat, I screamed again.

"Daniel!" Salt water filled my mouth. The waves flung bits of wood at me, and I ducked. Coral tore at my feet, but I pulled my lower limbs to my stomach, hoping the waves would toss me over the majority of the coral and dump me into the lagoon.

A soft dark shape bumped into me, and I grabbed Mrs. Darymple.

"Let go!" she screamed.

"I've got you. I'm a strong swimmer. Just tuck your knees to protect yourself, Mrs. Darymple!"

Sputtering a mouthful of salt water, she nodded and stopped resisting.

"Where is Mrs. Simpson?" I shouted. "Did you see her?"

"No, I have not seen her!"

I held on to Mrs. Darymple and tried to search for the others above the swirling froth but could see nothing. I thought I heard shouts, but that could have been the pounding of my pulse in my soggy ears.

"We've got to get out of this! Swim!"

I struck out in the direction of the waves with my right arm, pulling Mrs. Darymple with my left. She must have kicked, because her weight lightened.

We rose up on a wave again as if we were body surfing, and it dumped us into another mass of painful coral. I suspected my feet were bleeding, and I hoped the lagoon was free of sharks.

But the waves had also deposited us inside the turquoise lagoon, and my feet touched soft sand. The water level came to my waist.

"We're out of the waves. You can stand now." I let go of Mrs. Darymple and turned to look at the reef behind me.

Bits and pieces of lumber swirled in the surf, while others floated in the calm lagoon. My heart swelled with joy when I saw Daniel's dark head emerge from the froth. He had hold of Thomas and Mrs. Simpson.

"Daniel! Daniel!" I screeched, jumping up and down.

"Ouch!" I said, stepping on a piece of coral. "Look, Mrs. Darymple! Daniel has Mrs. Simpson!"

To Daniel's left, Frederick, James and Samuel swam into the lagoon, and I realized thankfully that our little group had survived.

Daniel waded through water toward us, half carrying a confused and whimpering Mrs. Simpson. Thomas walked beside them, casting worried glances at the older woman. They reached us, and Mrs. Darymple moved to take charge of her companion.

I wanted to throw myself against Daniel in joy, but the moment was lost when Thomas appeared at my side. I hugged him instead. The thin boy stiffened, and I let him go. His reddened cheeks suggested he wasn't used to being hugged.

"Where are we?" Mrs. Darymple asked.

We turned in unison to look at the island. Irregularly shaped jagged green peaks towered over the island, the tallest ones buried in low-hanging clouds. The whole image was mystical, like something out of a Hollywood movie.

"I have no idea," Daniel said. "None at all. Come. Let us wade to shore in case there are sharks in the lagoon."

At that, poor Mrs. Simpson whimpered again.

"Sharks?"

"Courage, Agatha. You must find courage," Mrs. Darymple said, not unkindly. "We are still alive!"

"I am trying," Mrs. Simpson said in a faltering voice.

"The island looks very small," I said, trying to step carefully over the coral bits in the sand as I waded in. "Ouch!"

"What is it?" Daniel said, moving near me.

"I keep stepping on coral! My feet are screaming in pain."

"That is right! You have no shoes!"

"No," I murmured, taking another tentative step forward.

"Come," Daniel said, and to my surprise, he swept me up into his arms. I melted in his embrace, forgetting for a brief moment that we were quite possibly stranded on a strange island or that many people had probably lost their lives.

The last thought sobered me, and I bit my lip as I wrapped my arms around Daniel's neck. He lowered me to the ground as he reached shore, and I ran my hands through the silky-feeling black sand.

"This is from lava, isn't it?" I asked. I buried my burning feet in the cool wet sand, which seemed to soothe them a bit.

Daniel, arms on his hips, studied the peaks. "Yes, I should think so. This is obviously a volcanic island, but I suspect from the peaks that its volcano is dormant. If it were active, the mountains would be softly rounded from lava flow."

"You know a lot about geology for a medical doctor."

Daniel looked down at me.

"An interest of mine."

"Thank goodness," Mrs. Darymple said on reaching shore. She set Mrs. Simpson down on shore next to me and turned to survey the beach. "A lovely spot under other circumstances."

I agreed with her. We had been shipwrecked in paradise. I only hoped civilization was nearby. Then I looked up at Daniel, standing by me, his black hair wet, white shirt plastered to his muscular chest, and I didn't seem to care. Paradise was anywhere near Daniel. As far as I was concerned, paradise was at his side.

I looked out toward the turquoise lagoon and wondered when I had fallen in love.

CHAPTER SIX

I was interrupted from my odd reverie by the arrival of the three crew members who had finally reached shore and dropped down onto the sand next to Mrs. Simpson. The boundary lines between passenger and crew had been dissolved, and rightly so.

"Coconuts," I said, looking up at the palm trees. "No matter what we find or don't find on this island, we'll always have something to eat and drink."

"Aye," Frederick said. "I worked in the kitchen. I can prepare a few things with the meat and milk of the coconut."

"Good man," Daniel said. "I am hopeless with a pot and pan, not that we have either. Do you know how to set a fire? We have plenty of lava rock to serve as a flint."

Fredrick pushed himself off the black sand and stood to look around.

"I think we can do something with the coconut husk and some of the rock. Should I set a fire now?"

"Yes, please do so that the ladies do not take chill," said Daniel, the de facto leader of our little group. "The rest of us will explore the island. Samuel and James, head west along the coast, and report back with what you find. Thomas and I will explore east."

"I want to go. I don't need to dry off!"

All eyes turned and surveyed me from head to toe. I looked down at the wet flowered island dress that clung to my curves. Crossing my arms over my chest, I cleared my throat.

"I'm almost dry. I'd like to go," I reiterated with burning cheeks.

"Mrs. Wollam, your feet took a severe beating on the coral," Daniel said. "I think I should wrap your feet up and that you should rest."

I looked up at Daniel, stunned by his formal use of my last name. He had been calling me Maggie. What had happened? Had I misunderstood the closeness between us?

I dropped my eyes and unearthed one of my feet to study the bleeding and raw sole. Daniel was right. I probably couldn't walk far and would probably only hinder them.

"Okay," I said with a sigh. "I'll huddle with the ladies here on the beach."

While Frederick gathered things to start a fire, Daniel picked me up to carry me to a dryer part of the beach, above the tide line. The two older women followed us, while James and Samuel headed down the beach on their mission to explore.

Daniel knelt in front of me and examined my feet. The wounds, still raw, had not yet started to clot, and blood continued to ooze from them.

"I am concerned with infection," he murmured. "I have no salve though."

"I'm pretty tough," I said, more to reassure him. "I'll be all right."

"I still need to wrap them." He sat back and looked around, as if for a bandage.

"Here," I said. I grabbed the hem of my dress and pulled it apart at the seam to tear off a few inches.

"Is she tearing her gown?" Mrs. Simpson whispered to Mrs. Darymple.

"I do not think she means to be immodest, Mrs. Simpson," Mrs. Darymple said dryly. "She needs bandages for her feet. Would you have the doctor give up his shirt?"

"No, of course not," Mrs. Simpson continued to whisper, though her voice carried.

Daniel drew in a heavy sigh and took the material from me.

"I would have given up my shirt," he said in a low voice meant only for my ears. He brushed sand from my feet before carefully wrapping them.

"You'll need it," I said thickly. The sensation of Daniel's hands on my feet transported me away from the people surrounding us and onto a tropical island all our own. I closed my eyes and imagined his hands on my face, around my waist, over my heart.

"There," he said in a husky voice. He cleared his throat and stood quickly.

Brought swiftly back to reality, I jerked my eyes open and looked up at Daniel.

"Stay off your feet, Mrs. Wollam. Ask Frederick if you need anything."

"Come, Thomas," he said briskly. They walked away, and I stared after them. I didn't want to let Daniel out of my sight. For all I knew, the island was inhabited by headhunters or tribes who still engaged in human sacrifice or—"

"Daniel!" I shrieked, scrambling to my feet but falling back in pain.

He pivoted and hurried back to my side.

"What is it? Is it your feet? Please stay off of them." He bent over me. When he would have straightened, I clutched at his arm.

"Please be careful. You don't know what's out there."

"Yes, of course, Maggie," he said. He threw the others a quick glance before running his fingers lightly across my jawline.

"I will only be gone a few hours at the most, I promise."

"Okay. Good. Don't call me Mrs. Wollam. So formal. It confuses me. Yes, go. I'm sorry," I murmured.

"No need to be sorry. I am flattered that you're worried about me. About us." He nodded toward Thomas, who waited for him some distance away.

"Maggie," Daniel whispered before walking away. I followed their progress wistfully until they disappeared from sight.

By now Frederick had a roaring fire going with the help of dried coconut husks and palm leaves. At that moment, he was busily paring open the top of several coconuts. He offered them to us to drink.

Mrs. Darymple and I took the water gratefully and drank it.

"Oh, no. No, I do not think I want to drink that," Mrs. Simpson said fretfully.

"Nonsense, Agatha! Drink," Mrs. Darymple ordered. "You must keep up your strength. We do not know if the island has any fresh water."

Mrs. Simpson reluctantly took the coconut Frederick offered her and sipped from it with a pinched face. I didn't know if she didn't like it or had decided she wasn't going to like it. Either way, she didn't drink much and set it aside.

"I'm sure one of them will find a fresh-water source," I said. "If not, we can collect rainwater somehow." I looked over my shoulder at the thick vegetation behind us.

"Perhaps this island is inhabited," Mrs. Darymple offered.

"Inhabited?" Mrs. Simpson said. "By whom? What if the island is inhabited by savages who eat people? I have heard of them."

"Agatha, dear, please stop spouting such nonsense," Mrs. Darymple said dryly.

I cleared my throat and looked away with burning cheeks. I feared the same thing myself, but I wasn't about to tell the ladies that.

"It's not nonsense." She sniffed. "I have heard of cannibalism in these islands."

"What islands, dear? We do not even know where we are!"

"The boys and I won't let anything happen to you, Mrs. Simpson. Be assured of that!" Frederick said.

"See, Agatha? We have four men to see after us," Mrs. Darymple said. She followed that with a sigh. "I wonder how that very pleasant man, Mr. Asher, fared."

I wondered about all the passengers. Would more wash up on shore? Alive? I didn't want to think about the alternative.

"Frederick, will they send a search party out once they discover the ship went down?" I asked. Of course, there was no chance that we'd be discovered by satellites, or even airplanes—not in the mid-nineteenth century.

"It could be a week or more before anyone notices that the *Vigilance* failed to arrive in Tahiti, Mrs. Wollam. While other ships in the region might search for signs of the *Vigilance*, I do not think the owners of the shipping company will send out an organized search party of other ships. We do not know where we are. The company can have no idea where we are."

"I wonder if we should keep the fire going anyway, in case a ship passes by," I said. "They might be able see the smoke."

"As could other persons who might be on the island," Mrs. Simpson said darkly.

"Oh dear, Agatha," Mrs. Darymple began. "You utter those words in such an ominous voice. If there other are people on the island, they might be very friendly, welcoming sorts who wish only to help us."

"From your lips," Mrs. Simpson said.

"We shall see when the men return," Mrs. Darymple said. "In the meantime, my dress is quite dry and the fire is making me sleepy. I might just rest for a bit. I am quite exhausted."

"I shall join you," Mrs. Simpson said. "I do so wish I had a blanket though."

"We shall have to make do for now, Agatha."

The ladies lay down, and I eyed a few palm fronds nearby. I suspected I could make some sort of basket from the stiffest leaves, but could I weave some bedding for the women?

Frederick busied himself with more coconuts, and I rose and hobbled over to collect a few fronds. To my dismay, my feet hurt far more than when I had first reached the beach, and I suspected they were swelling. Despite what I had said to Daniel, I too hoped they wouldn't get infected. It didn't matter if I was in the nineteenth century or the twenty-first century—I had no access to antibiotics.

Frederick came to my rescue when he saw me trying to reach palm leaves, and he helped me pull down various textures.

I spent the next hour weaving some of the softer leaves together, and when I'd managed a square of about five feet by five feet, I got Frederick to help me lay it gently over the ladies. It didn't mold cozily to their forms like a blanket, but I hoped it would at least keep the sea breezes off their bodies while they slept. And if nothing else, they could use it as a mat to sleep on in the future.

I settled myself again and watched the turquoise lagoon as the ladies slept. Even Frederick, having husked about a dozen coconuts, dozed, but I fought to keep my eyes open. I didn't know what would happen if I fell asleep, but I wasn't ready to return to the future. I couldn't possibly leave Daniel at that moment, never to know how his life would turn out.

Daniel and Thomas were the first to return, and I jumped up when I saw them but fell back again when pain shot through my feet. If anything, my feet hurt even worse than they had just a few hours prior. I gritted my teeth, smiled and pretended that I chose to sit and watch their approach along the beach.

They returned alone, with all their body parts intact, thankfully, but with no signs that they had encountered civilization. They carried nothing with them and looked hot and tired when they threw themselves down beside me.

Frederick awakened and handed them each a coconut to drink.

"What did you find?" I asked.

"Nothing. The island is small in circumference, only about five miles at its widest point as far as I can see. We were prevented from circumnavigating the entire coast by a sheer cliff at one point. I assume James and Samuel will have encountered the same obstacle if they traveled that far."

"So you didn't see anyone else? The island is uninhabited?"

"It would appear so. Are you well?" Daniel asked. "Did anything happen while we were gone?"

"No, nothing," I said. "As you can see, Samuel and James haven't returned yet. The ladies have been sleeping."

At my words, Mrs. Darymple sat up, staring down at the woven mat I had made.

"What is this?"

"Mrs. Wollam made it," Frederick said. "To protect you from the wind."

"How very clever," Mrs. Darymple said, fingering the weaving.

I blushed.

"You will have to teach me your techniques so that Mrs. Simpson and I can weave some mats and perhaps some baskets. From what I heard of your conversation, Dr. Hawthorne, we are going to need to fend for ourselves, is that true? We are quite alone?"

"Yes, I believe that is the case. We must find a fresh-water supply, perhaps further inland. The boys can fashion some fishing implements. We will build some shelters. Those will be our first priorities."

I stared at my feet, wondering how I was going to be able to help. Daniel must have read my mind.

"How are your feet? Let me have a look at them."

Daniel knelt in front of me and carefully unwrapped my bandages, which partially stuck to the clotting blood on my wounds. His gentle touch swelled my heart. I felt no pain when he explored my injuries, though in reality, I knew that they hurt.

"My poor dear," Mrs. Darymple said. "Your feet look absolutely dreadful!"

"I know. They do look awful, don't they?" I confirmed. "I'm afraid they feel as bad as they look."

"I found something that I think will help," Daniel said as he reached into a pocket of his trousers and withdrew a bundled handkerchief. He opened it to reveal a handful of broad green leaves on stalks.

"Leaves from a breadfruit tree," he said. "The sap is known for its healing properties." He squeezed the severed end of each stalk and allowed a thick milky liquid to drip over the soles of my feet before carefully massaging the sap into my wounds. A soothing coolness began to spread over the cuts, and I smiled.

"It does feel better!"

"Good," he said. He looked up. "Ah! Samuel and James have returned. What do they have in their hands?"

Samuel and James approached from the west side of the island, carrying armfuls of what appeared to be small bananas, little red-and-green apple-pear-like fruits and branches of some sort of red berries. Clearly we would be eating a lot of fruit in the near future.

Daniel, Frederick and Thomas rose to relieve them of their burdens.

"Well done, boys!" Daniel said.

By now, Mrs. Simpson had awakened and sat up. I heard Mrs. Darymple explaining my version of a blanket to her. Frederick commandeered the fruit and began preparing a meal with the ingredients at hand.

Activity picked up as the men moved toward the tree line, discussing various woods and how best to fashion some fishing gear. Mrs. Darymple and Mrs. Simpson disappeared into another part of the jungle for a hygienic visit. I watched the activity around me feeling a bit helpless, given my injured feet. For all that I had come from the twenty-first century, I seemed to have no advanced knowledge that could help those of us stranded on an island in the South Pacific.

CHAPTER SEVEN

The men built four A-line huts just inside the tree line with loose timber and palm fronds. Given the size of the shelters, Daniel had decided that they could hold only two people comfortably, a choice that pleased me to no end. I really didn't want to share a hut with the ladies. I didn't really know them, nor they me. They most certainly didn't know that I had traveled through time.

I no longer believed that I was dreaming. It just didn't make sense. The catalyst for the time travel appeared to be sleep, and it had been natural to assume that my visits to the nineteenth century were nothing more than dreams, but I had slept since then on the skiff. And I hadn't traveled back to the twenty-first century.

No, as fantastical as it seemed, I had traveled in time, and I didn't know why. Perhaps I would never know why, or how.

I was interrupted from my reverie by the return of the ladies.

"Do show us how to weave these palms, Mrs. Wollam," Mrs. Darymple said.

"Maggie, please."

"Maggie then," she agreed. I didn't ask Mrs. Darymple for her first name because I doubted I would ever use it. I felt certain the ladies would always be Mrs. Darymple and Mrs. Simpson to me.

After a cursory lesson in palm-frond weaving, the ladies and I made matting for the sloped roofs of the A-frames as well as wall coverings and flooring. Additionally, we wove a few more blanket-style coverings from the softer palm leaves I had found.

Frederick kept the fire stoked, and by evening we had the beginnings of a small village. At some point in the afternoon, James and Samuel, armed with empty coconut shells, had ventured inland to find a fresh-water source. They discovered a nearby waterfall and pool and returned with as much water as they could carry.

****

Daniel and Thomas had tried their hand at fishing with a makeshift spear, and while they afforded us some humor, they were unsuccessful that time.

"Do not worry, Thomas," Daniel said, patting the boy on the shoulder. "We will ultimately succeed."

I smiled, but I was allergic to seafood, so their success at fishing didn't affect me. I had faith that Daniel would see to the health of the group and their diet. As for me, I had been wondering what I was going to eat while on the island. I would have to find some nuts for protein. Thankfully, there appeared to be fruit in abundance and apparently a fresh-water source. I supposed I should be grateful I hadn't gone on a cruise to Scandinavia.

The sun set on that first night sooner than we expected. The older ladies moved into their hut with the blanket I made them and settled in.

From my painfully slow but necessary retreat into the foliage behind our little encampment, I could hear them talking.

"I would love a cup of tea," I heard Mrs. Simpson saying. "And a change of clothing."

"Yes, I agree with you there, Agatha. Perhaps we can ask one of the men to take some of our clothing to the pool they found to wash out the salt."

"Our underthings?" Mrs. Simpson asked in a querulous voice. "Not a man surely."

"Well, I suppose *you* could wash our clothes then," Mrs. Darymple responded.

"Mrs. Darymple, how can I wash our things in a pond? I need hot water, a proper bucket and some soap."

"Agatha, how is it that you do not yet understand our circumstances? Our ship was sunk. We are stranded on an island in the South Pacific. No one is coming to our rescue as far as we know. We have only the clothes on our back and the food we find on the island. We simply must make do!"

"Perhaps that young woman might consent to wash our clothing?" Mrs. Simpson suggested. "Mrs. Wollam? Her vulgar dress suggests she is from the working class. Who is she anyway? Do you know?

Dr. Hawthorne seems overly familiar with her, would you not agree?"

I froze, crouched in midstream, holding my breath. My awkward position did nothing to improve the pain in my feet.

"I have no idea who Mrs. Wollam is or where she came from," Mrs. Darymple responded. "I had not seen her aboard the ship until last night. She may very well be the doctor's paramour. Who can say? I am quite sure it is not *my* place to inquire. Nor do I think it should be yours. I like the young woman. She seems very pleasant and has been quite solicitous to us. I do not believe she is a servant of any sort, but you are more than welcome to *try* and ask her to wash your clothing, Agatha. I would very much enjoy seeing that exchange!"

"Well, I am sure she is a *very* pleasant woman." Mrs. Simpson sounded as huffy as Mrs. Darymple intended. "Paramour indeed. How very shocking!"

"If our future lies on this island, Dr. Hawthorne and Mrs. Wollam may be the most fortunate among us. Now get some rest, Agatha. Tomorrow is a new day."

"Good night," Mrs. Simpson murmured.

I rose and hobbled back toward the entrance to my A-frame hut. A lone silhouette outlined against the sunset caught my attention. Daniel. I shuffled through the sand to his side.

Fiery-orange, the sun hovered just above the horizon, casting a halo of golden light across the clouds and a dazzling path of sparkling reddish highlights across the darkening purple sea. The wind had picked up and whistled through the air.

"Mrs. Darymple thinks I might be your paramour," I said with a chuckle. "Mrs. Simpson wonders if I'll wash their clothes for them."

Daniel turned to me. Even as the sun dropped below the horizon, it illuminated the shock on his face.

"No!"

"Oh, it's funny!" I reassured him. "Which shocks you more?"

"Both, I am afraid. I must correct Mrs. Darymple's impression as soon as possible."

"But not Mrs. Simpson? She believes I'm from the working class because my dress is vulgar."

"I cannot believe she said such! How very unkind of her. I quite like your gown. No, this will not do. I really must speak to the ladies in the morning."

"And how do you intend to explain me to them? If I'm not your paramour?"

As much as I wished that were true, I think I enjoyed watching the disapproving muscles twitch in Daniel's jaw.

"Please, Mrs. Wollam."

"I thought it was Maggie. Why do you switch to the more formal title? It's so confusing, and I never know where I stand with you!"

I said more than I meant.

"I apologize...Maggie. Yes, of course I shall call you Maggie in private, but given that the ladies are already suspicious of us, perhaps it is best I refer to you as Mrs. Wollam in public. And you must call me Daniel."

"I already do. We aren't quite as formal in the twenty-first century."

Daniel sighed. "No, I can see that you are not. As to the ladies, I am uncertain what I should say, but I cannot have them think ill of you or assume that you are some sort of washerwoman."

"To be fair, it was only Mrs. Simpson who thought I might be willing to do the laundry. Mrs. Darymple dared her to even ask."

"Still, why Mrs. Darymple would simply assume that you were—" Daniel stopped short.

"Your paramour?"

"Must you continue to say that word?"

"Is it really offensive in your time? I don't even think we use it anymore."

"Yes, it suggests—" He paused and cleared his throat. "It suggests intimacy without marriage."

I said nothing but turned to look at the sunset. My heart dropped to my stomach. I had quite liked the idea of becoming Daniel's paramour at some future point, especially if we were stranded on a tropical island for an indeterminate length of time. But the revulsion in Daniel's voice suggested he felt otherwise. I swallowed hard, knowing that I had mistaken the closeness between us. I had foolishly fantasized our relationship, imagining something that wasn't there.

"And I have too much respect for you to allow people to think such vile things about you."

"Vile?" I whispered, keeping my face fixed on the horizon.

"Yes, of course! Loathsome indeed. No, I really must speak to the women in the morning."

"That will be awkward," I murmured, trying to absorb the rejection I felt at his words, his tone. "I'll handle it. After all, I'm the one who overheard them talking."

"What will you say?"

"The truth." The words came out in a bitter tone. "That there is no chance of such a thing." I turned and hobbled away, ignoring Daniel's voice as he called out my name.

I crawled into my hut, wishing I could slam the door or close the curtain, but I had no such privacy. The men had not managed to fashion any sort of doorway, and so the huts were only three-sided. I huddled against one matted wall and listened to the wind blow. The temperature had dropped, and the air felt chill. I hugged myself, tucked my knees into my chest and did everything I could to stay awake. To fall asleep might throw me forward in time, and though Daniel didn't feel the same about me, I wasn't ready to leave him.

Time passed. I wasn't sure how much, perhaps an hour. The wind coming off the sea had begun to howl, and I heard nearby thumps and bumps. A round shape landed with a roll just in front of my hut, and I realized some of the noises I heard came from falling coconuts.

I scrambled to my knees and peered out of the hut toward the sea, hoping that a hurricane wasn't imminent. But the air, while moist, held no rain. The waves, visible in the moonlight, sounded peaceful enough.

"Maggie?" a voice whispered. Daniel appeared at the opening of the hut. He crouched down to peer at me. "Are you all right?"

"Yes, I'm fine. The wind picked up, and I was afraid a storm was coming in."

He turned to look toward the water. "Everything appears calm, although the winds have grown stronger with nightfall, that is true."

"Yes," I murmured. "Haven't you slept? You need to sleep."

"No, I have not. Did you?"

I didn't answer for a moment.

"No."

"What are you trying to do?"

"What do you mean?" I asked.

"Are you trying to stay awake to avoid traveling back in time?" he whispered.

"What?" Of course I knew what he was asking, but I pretended not to understand.

"You know what I am asking, Maggie. Why did you not sleep?"

"I guess I'm not sleepy."

"Maggie!"

"I'm not ready to leave." I gave in.

"You must if you can," Daniel said. "There is no point in you remaining here."

"No point?"

"None."

Tears streamed down my face.

"You don't have to hit me over the head with it, you know."

"What?"

"I know what you mean."

"And what do I mean?"

"That you want me to go."

"I do want you to go, Maggie. This is no place for you. If you have the ability to leave, then you must go. Return to your life."

"Sure! And then I'll send a rescue ship for you all," I muttered.

"Maggie," he remonstrated.

"Oh, wait! That won't work, will it?"

"I fear not. I am unsure why you wish to stay, but at some point, you will have to sleep."

"You're unsure why I want to stay," I repeated in a flat voice.

"Please do not say that you are staying for me," he said, also in a flat voice. "I do not want you to stay on this island simply for me."

My throat constricted, and my heart burst into a thousand pieces. No more beating around the bush. He had told me he wanted me to leave.

"Please go away," I said. I turned my back on him.

"Maggie," he said.

"Just go. Leave!" Pain gripped my chest as I swallowed a sob. I couldn't even breathe with him there.

"I only want what is best for you," he said.

"Right! Good-bye!" I said, keeping my back to him.

I heard a heavy sigh, as if he was about to speak again, and I rose to my knees. Lifting the matting at the opposite end of my hut, I scrambled out the other side.

I hobbled into the underbrush, knowing he wouldn't follow since we had unofficially set the area off as a restroom. I didn't get far in the dark but dropped down into the sand, against the trunk of a fallen coconut tree, and I waited for Daniel to leave. I wasn't sure how I would know when that happened, as the wind and rustling in the foliage masked the sound of footsteps, but I gave it about five minutes. Then I limped toward the beach, bypassing my hut. I moved away from the encampment and dropped down on a likely spot on the sand at the water's edge.

Hugging my legs to my chest, I pressed my head on my knees and tried to reason through my angst. I realized that Daniel's desire to see me gone wasn't personal. He wanted the best for me, and to him, that was returning to the comforts of my time, where I probably would *not* be stranded on a tropical island.

Neither of us knew if that was the case, of course, but I doubted it. We seemed to have reached a mutual yet unspoken consensus that sleep was the catalyst for the time travel. And I couldn't stay awake forever. Already, my eyes threatened to close of their own accord. The wind washing over me combined with the rhythmic sound of the waves worked to make me drowsy.

Exhausted, I lay down in the sand and stared up at the moon. A bright beacon in any century, the round sphere grounded me. I let go and closed my eyes, unwilling to say good-bye to Daniel and unsure how to stay awake. If I could have drifted off in his arms...

Suddenly, I felt myself lifted. Hands slid under my shoulders and lifted my upper body.

"Daniel?"

I heard several men's hushed voices as I was hoisted into the air. I struggled and opened my mouth to scream, but a cloying sweet-smelling cloth came over my face, and I knew no more.

CHAPTER EIGHT

I awakened to dappled sunlight peeking through a massive banyan tree. Thick emerald-green jungle surrounded me. Birds chirped and flying bugs buzzed, and I swore I could hear the sound of a waterfall.

But I wasn't alone. Three men sat cross-legged in a circle near me, eating and speaking in low voices. Lying on my side, I froze, peeking at them through my lashes.

Long curly black hair hung down their backs in various styles. Each man sported some sort of facial hair. A majority of their semi-naked muscular bodies revealed myriad tattoos in varying Polynesian designs. All three men wore loincloths wrapped around their hips and over their genitals.

I couldn't make out their language, but what I did conclude was that the island was indeed inhabited by Polynesians. It remained to be seen what they planned to do with me.

Visions of being draped over a sacrificial altar terrified me, and I contemplated jumping up and running. Contemplated only. I knew I wouldn't get far on my injured feet or without any idea of where we were. The lithe men before me would surely manage to catch me before I got away.

My tongue felt thick and dry. The foul-sweet stench of the cloth they'd pressed over my face stayed with me.

I imagined Daniel waking and not finding me there. Would he think I'd fallen asleep and traveled forward in time? And the rest of the camp? Would they wonder if I'd walked into the sea? Been taken by a wild animal? I knew the group would try to look for me, but they might never suspect that I had been taken by humans.

If Daniel believed that I'd traveled back in time, he would be disinclined to look for me. He might even tell the group the truth about me and tell them not to worry, that I was in a good place, safe in the twenty-first century.

I peeked at the Polynesians again from under my eyelashes. Each one carried at least one weapon of some sort attached to his waist—knives, a small ax, a wooden club. My heart stopped. What if they had slaughtered Daniel and the others?

No! I couldn't bear the thought. No!

I pushed myself up to a sitting position, and the three men jumped to their feet, as if to prevent me from fleeing.

"Where are they? Did you kill them?" I begged in a raspy voice. "Please tell me you didn't kill them."

I saw no sign of blood on their hands, their bodies, their weapons, but that proved nothing. I had no idea how long I'd been unconscious. It could have been hours, even days. They could have cleaned up long before I awakened.

Of similar heights and stocky builds, the men looked at each other when I spoke, as if they didn't understand my words. One who appeared to be in in his early twenties spoke to me. I gathered he was speaking some form of Polynesian, though I thought I recognized a French word or two, but I couldn't be sure.

"I don't speak French," I said with an agitated shake of my head. "Did you kill them? My friends. Did you kill them?"

The one who appeared to be in charge of the group drew his dark brows together and shook his head, again as if he didn't understand what I was saying. Lustrous black eyes stared at me. High cheekbones dominated an extraordinarily handsome face.

What was the French word for kill, murder? I didn't know, couldn't think.

"*Vous morte? Morte?*" What was I saying? Did that mean death? Would they think I was asking if they were going to kill me? That too!

The exchanged a few words, and the young one rattled off a bunch of words to me. All I could do was shake my head again.

"*Vous morte ami? Mes mi?*" I tried hard to recall any French words I'd ever heard. At this, the young one's face broke into a smile, and he spoke to the others. They laughed and shook their heads.

"*Non,*" the young one said. He pointed to his chest. "Kai-hau."

Relief flooded through me. "*Non*" sounded a lot like none, even no.

I thought he was saying that they hadn't killed Daniel and the others.

Kaihau pointed to me and shrugged his shoulders in what I interpreted as an inquiry. Surely they weren't planning on killing me if they wanted to know my name, right?

"Maggie Wollam," I said.

"Ma-gee," Kaihau repeated. The other men tried my name out as well. Kaihau touched each one on the chest and introduced them as "Aikane" and "Posoa." Aikane and Posoa also appeared to be in their twenties and shared such similar features that I found it hard to tell them apart.

Kaihau bent and picked up a banana, which he unpeeled and handed to me. I was more thirsty than hungry, and I made what I thought was a universal gesture of drinking. Kaihau smiled, his teeth bright white and even, and he motioned for me to follow him.

I pushed myself to a standing position and started to hobble after him but cried out in pain. My feet hurt worse than they had before, if that was possible. I looked down at them. Even my ankles were swollen.

Kaihau swung around to look at me and then at my bandaged feet. He motioned to Aikane and Posoa, who moved toward me. They locked arms and nodded that I should climb into the chair they formed. Feeling very foolish but less fearful of the Polynesians, given their solicitous behavior, I sat down and let them carry me toward the sound of the water.

We emerged onto the sight of a tall, slender waterfall slipping over a black lava rock ledge before dropping into a small stream. Aikane and Posoa carried me to the edge of the stream and set me down on a rock.

Kaihau grabbed a broad leaf from a plant, folded it and bent to fill it with water, which he then handed to me. I had already conceded that filtered water was a thing of the past—or future—and I accepted the makeshift cup gratefully and drank the cool water.

The Polynesians watched me and talked among themselves. I understood nothing of what they were saying, but they seemed like very genial men. Why had they taken me? Surely such amiable islanders didn't really intend to sacrifice me, did they? Or worse? No, I didn't sense that they eyed me with lust or had plans to abuse me.

Satiated, I patted some water on my face and stared at the waterfall, wondering if I we were still close to the encampment. Could I scream? Dared I?

Kaihau said something, and Aikane and Posoa approached me. Once again, they locked arms, and I meekly stepped into the chair, folding my hands in my lap. Screaming for help was out of the question, and I settled in to see where they planned on taking me.

We traveled for hours without stopping. The gentle bouncing put me to sleep a few times, and I awakened to find my head lolling on either Aikane's or Posoa's shoulders. I jerked straight, and they smiled. All in all, the journey should have been a girl's dream, being toted by two handsome bare-chested men.

The thick foliage of the jungle suggested the absence of a well-traveled path, and I doubted that Daniel or the other men would ever find a trace of us to follow. The Polynesians knew where they were going, but they left little trace of our journey. Whatever grasses they trampled sprung up again right away. If the men parted trees to pass through, the leaves sprung together again immediately.

I had to remind myself once again that Daniel might not even suspect I had been kidnapped, that he probably assumed I had fallen asleep and disappeared in time. I suspected now that sleep wasn't the only catalyst for the time travel. I had been well and truly unconscious for some time after the Polynesians had taken me, and I hadn't returned to my own time.

We emerged onto the top of a cliff. The sea lay before us, sparkling azure blue under the sun. I recognized the descriptions of the sheer cliff that stopped Daniel and the others from circumnavigating the island via the beach.

Far down below, a pale turquoise bay nestled in between the black lava rock cliffs, effectively cutting the area off from the rest of the island. Numerous outrigger canoes dotted the shoreline. Partially visible through the trees below was a complex of round thatched-roof huts. A village, I presumed. I saw people moving around, children playing.

Kaihau pointed to the village.

"Leakiki," he said.

"Leakiki," I repeated. Kaihau nodded. I wondered how we were going to get down to the village, and I held my breath as Aikane and Posoa handily carried me along a steep, narrow path known along the cliff face, dropping in increments until they emerged onto a lawn of mixed sand and native grass.

The villagers, who had seemed so small from the top of the cliff, spotted us and moved forward to examine me with curiosity. Young and old, tall and short, they uniformly wore lengths of material in various configurations, the women more modestly than the men. The women accessorized their long, luxurious wavy hair with brilliant colorful flowers, while both sexes sported jewelry fashioned from dark nuts, flowers and grasses. Tattooed bodies were common, even on the women. Shoes were apparently not necessary

A tiny wizened older woman, long curly gray hair flowing down her back, faded-red sarong tied around her neck in a figure eight, approached us, eyeing me carefully. Aikane and Posoa set me down onto the ground in a sitting position.

She moved toward me and reached out to touch my face. Her gentle touch didn't threaten me, and I remained still. She looked up at Kaihau and spoke. I didn't understand what she said, but she seemed disturbed. Not so much angry as disapproving.

Kaihau answered her in a respectful tone, but he didn't seem cowed. He pointed to me at certain points in their conversation.

I felt the eyes of the people upon me as Kaihau and the older woman talked. Not at all menacing, some even smiled at me. The older woman turned and called out something to the crowd. A beautiful young woman hurried up to join us. Like many of the young people, her dark hair matched the lustrous blackness of her eyes. She wore a dark-blue sarong modestly over one shoulder, toga style.

The older woman talked to her for a moment before she turned to me.

"My name Losa," the younger woman said in halting English tinged with a French accent. "Your name?" She gestured elegantly toward me.

"You speak English!" I cried out. "Maggie Wollam!"

She nodded, her full lips curving into a friendly smile.

"Yes, English missionary teach. You welcome here," she said. "This grandmother Rimu. That brother Kaihau. Cousin Posoa. That Aikane."

"Thank you," I said. "Why did they kidnap me? Do you know? Are my friends okay? Did they hurt them?"

The older woman said something, and Losa responded to her. Losa then turned to her brother, and it seemed as if they exchanged a few sharp words. Kaihau pointed to me a few times, and I knew I was at the center of their discussion. He waved a dismissive hand and stalked off.

Losa returned her attention to me.

"You friends no hurt. Sleeping. Kaihau take you for trade."

"Trade!" I barely heard her assurance that Daniel and the others were okay as I pushed myself up to stand on my feet. Pain shot through my soles, and I wobbled and grabbed Losa for support.

"You hurt!" She looked down at my feet, then spoke to the older woman.

"What do you mean, trade?" I interrupted. "Trade me to whom? What's going on?"

"Grandmother fix you feet," she said. "Come." She gestured toward Posoa and Aikane, who picked me up again in the chair. They carried me toward a hut situated on a slight mound above the village and deposited me inside on a woven reed mat covering much of the floor.

"Losa! Who are they going to trade me to? Why?"

The men backed out of the hut, leaving me with Rimu and Losa. Losa spoke to Rimu, who crouched over some pots and clay jars, busily sorting through them.

Losa turned back to me.

"Grandmother fix feet. Then talk."

Rimu, finding what she needed, approached me with a jar. She removed my bandages carefully and examined my feet, now inflamed and oozing. Rimu tsked at the sight of them, and I gasped in pain as she slathered some sort of purple ointment on the soles. She rewrapped them using the same material and pointed to my dress. I nodded, assuming she asked if I'd used the dress for bandaging.

Rimu sat back, and I turned to Losa with my previous question.

"What do you mean trade? What are they going to do with me?"

Losa and Rimu spoke for a moment before Losa turned to me.

"Brother trade you French."

"What? To the French? Why would they want me?"

"Maybe French no want you. Kaihau want Vana back."

"Vana? What's Vana?"

"Vana his woman?"

"Girlfriend? Wife?"

Losa scrunched her face. "No wife."

"Girlfriend?"

Losa shrugged her shoulders with a shake of her head, giving me the impression she didn't understand the word. I dropped the relationship to focus on the main issue.

"So the French, whoever they are, have Kaihau's girlfriend, for some reason, and he intends to trade me to them in exchange for her?"

I could tell from Losa's expression that I had used far too many words for her to translate and follow, not to mention the high pitch in my anxious voice probably distorted my words.

"Yes?" she responded uncertainly.

I wanted to jump up and run, but my crippled feet continued to trap me. The pain had lessened thanks to whatever ointment Rimu had slathered on them, but I doubted I could walk, much less run.

"That's barbaric!" I almost shouted. "No! He can't. No!" I sputtered.

Losa's face drooped, and she turned to Rimu. They spoke and both shook their heads, regarding me with obvious sympathy.

"I no like. Tell Kaihau. No one stop him."

"Can't Rimu or an elder tell him no? Won't he listen?" My pulse raced as I pled.

"Kaihau chief. Father die one year before. No one say no to chief."

I closed my eyes, trying to calm the rising hysteria that threatened to erupt into a scream. Kaihau had seemed so kind. I couldn't believe he would simply turn me over to strangers. I didn't even understand the implications of being turned over to the French.

"Do you mean missionaries? Like French priests?"

Losa shook her head. "No missionary. Sailor?"

"Sailors?" The implications terrified me. Kaihau planned to turn me over to French sailors. No, that sounded horrendous. I desperately wished that Daniel knew where I was, wished that he could save me from a fate that terrified me.

"What will the French do with me?" My voice shook.

Losa turned and spoke to Rimu again. Rimu's response was brief, and she looked away.

"Rimu say French take you for wife. Sorry." Losa's lustrous eyes glistened with sympathy as she laid a warm hand on my cold arm. The interior of the hut darkened for a moment before I released the air I'd been holding. I recovered from faintness and dragged in a deep gulp of air.

"No," I whispered, as if withholding my consent was a possibility.

Losa dropped her eyes.

"When does he plan on trading me?" If I could possibly return to the twenty-first century, now was the time. I willed it to be so.

"French come tomorrow. Kaihau trade you for Vana."

"Tomorrow?" I squeaked. I didn't have much time.

CHAPTER NINE

I don't know who decided that I would stay in Rimu's hut that night, but stay I did. Losa stayed there as well, and I guessed that she lived with her grandmother. And just to make sure I didn't decide to wander away in the night, even if I could have walked any great length, Aikane had been posted at the door of the hut.

While I racked my brain trying to figure out how to escape from my captors, I noted that Aikane and Losa gazed at each other often. At any other time, I would have thought they would make a cute couple, but at that moment I didn't care.

Rimu and Losa busied themselves with prepping food throughout the afternoon, which they delivered to Posoa and Kaihau, who had returned. Through the open door, I could see that the men cooked food in some sort of pit. I watched the smoke rise, wondering if there was any chance Daniel might see it and come for me. Then I reminded myself yet again that he would most likely think I had traveled back in time. He wouldn't know to rescue me.

"Can I talk to Kaihau?" I asked Losa.

She nodded with a sympathetic expression and left the hut to go outside to speak to her brother. With a sick feeling in my stomach, I saw Kaihau's expression as he looked toward the hut. I didn't know him, but his expression looked determined. Nevertheless, he left the pit and followed Losa into the hut. He seated himself cross-legged across from me and waited.

"Please ask your brother to return me to where he found me, to my friends."

Losa gave her head a quick shake and opened her mouth as

if to argue with me, but I leaned forward and pleaded.

"Please, Losa, just ask him."

She hesitated and then turned to her brother. I understood only one word of the exchange, and that was *amis*, the French word for friends, giving me some confidence that Losa was passing along my request.

Kaihau eyed me, smiled politely and gave a firm shake of his head. He began to rise, and I spoke quickly.

"Please, Kaihau, please don't do this! Let me speak to the French when they come. Let me tell them how wrong it is to take women. Is it even legal? Maybe I can shame them into giving Vana back."

Kaihau scrunched his dark eyebrows together and looked from me to Losa. I knew Losa didn't understand half of what I said, and I bit my lips.

"Please don't trade me," I said slowly. "I will speak to the French. Ask for Vana."

Losa translated for me, and Kaihau shook his head again and said something to his sister. She turned to me with a shrug.

"Kaihau say try. French say no, he trade you."

I thought I understood her words. I would be allowed to talk to the French, if I could even communicate with them, but if they didn't give Vana back voluntarily, then Kaihau would offer me in exchange.

"Okay," I acquiesced, fervently hoping I could reason with the traders. "You speak some French, Losa, right? Will you translate tomorrow for me?"

I could see she didn't understand.

"Will you speak to the French for me?"

A look of shock clouded her face, and she shook her head.

"No!" she said sharply.

"What?" I asked, my own voice strident. "Why not? What if they don't speak English? How can I talk to them?"

Kaihau interrupted, no doubt asking what we were talking about. Losa turned to him and said something. At this, the previously silent Rimu spoke up. I couldn't make out her words, but she seemed distressed, waving her hands. Kaihau shook his head firmly, spoke loudly and with a gesture urged his sister to translate his words.

"No," she repeated. "French come—girls hide now."

"Oh!" I said, easing out a tense breath. "Yes, of course. I understand. Maybe one of them speaks English."

Losa nodded, though I wasn't sure if she was validating my statement or just acknowledging it.

"Would the captain speak English?"

She shrugged her shoulders and turned to Kaihau with the question. He shrugged his shoulders as well.

"Speak French," Losa said.

I hoped she didn't mean me.

"The captain speaks French?" I clarified.

"Yes." She nodded.

Kaihau, apparently not one for sitting very long, rose. I threw him one last beseeching look to abandon his idea altogether, but he pretended not to see me. He left the hut. Suddenly claustrophobic and feeling trapped, I tried to rise to go outside and get some fresh air, but Rimu gently pushed me back down.

I settled back down on my woven mat and stared morosely out of the hut door, watching the men who knelt over the heavily smoking pit to peer into its contents. Escape was an impossibility, at least in the foreseeable future, especially crippled as I was.

The men soon joined Rimu, Losa and me for a dinner served in wooden bowls. The food smelled delicious, fragrant and enticing, but I ate nothing. My stomach felt as if it were gripped in a vice, and I couldn't relax. Aikane and Posoa, probably aware of my pleas, diplomatically ignored me, as did Kaihau. The Polynesians generally spoke among themselves.

"Food good?" Losa asked.

I nodded.

"Yes, very good. Thank you!"

She nodded and returned her attention to the conversation with her family. Since I caught no sideways glances in my direction, I assumed I wasn't a topic, and for that, I was glad.

Late afternoon darkened into evening, and the men rose to leave. I gathered then that Kaihau didn't live with his sister and grandmother. I noted another exchange of glances between Aikane and Losa before Aikane returned to his post outside the door.

"Sleep now," Losa said as she settled down on a woven mat across the hut. Rimu's gentle snoring indicated she had already fallen asleep near Losa.

I lay awake listening to the sound of the waves on the beach, now audible as the village uniformly seemed to quiet down for the night. Even the birds had grown silent. I closed my eyes and wished myself back in the twenty-first century, repeating a mantra over and over in my head.

Send me back. I'll miss Daniel so much. Send me back. I'll never see Daniel again. Send me back. Send me back.

At some point, I drifted off.

"Maggie," a voice said softly. Warm fingers caressed my cheek, and I opened my eyes. Moonlight shone through the open doorway of the hut and centered on the face of the man kneeling beside me.

"Daniel?" I whispered. My pulse pounded as I pushed myself upright. "Daniel?"

"Shhhh," he said, putting a finger to his lips.

I looked around the hut and saw that Rimu and Losa still slept.

"How did you find me?"

"Foolish girl," Daniel said. "You are as a beacon to me. I could find you anywhere."

My heart leapt at his romantic words. I wrapped my arms around his neck, and he lifted me in one fluid motion.

"They're going to trade me to the French," I whispered. "Please get me out of here."

"Yes, of course. No one will take you from me."

I melted in Daniel's arms. Safe, secure and fearing nothing, I clung to him as he moved toward the door.

Aikane slept just outside the doorway. The moon, full, round and bright, glowed down on the seaside village. In the distance, I thought I saw a mass of white sails flutter in the bay, the sails of a large ship approaching.

"The French!" I whispered. "They're here! Look!" I pointed out to sea.

Daniel paused to follow my hand.

"A ship!" he said. "Our way off the island! We cannot leave the village now. I must stay and see if they'll give us passage!"

I jerked and looked up at Daniel's face.

"What? No! Didn't you hear me? They're going to trade me to the French for a captive."

"Do not worry, my love! I will not let that happen."

My heart should have swelled at the endearment, but I could only focus on Daniel's odd behavior.

"Daniel! These people are not going to let me go. I already asked. The chief wants his girlfriend back, and he thinks he can trade me for her."

Daniel stood frozen, holding me, staring out to sea. I wasn't a heavy carry, but he didn't seem to be struggling with my weight.

"Daniel?"

He continued to stare out to sea, his eyes wide and fixed.

"Daniel?" I whispered again. I blinked and opened my eyes to the sight of moonlight filtering into the door of the hut. With a gasp, I pushed myself up and looked around.

"Daniel?" I whispered.

But Daniel wasn't there. Rimu and Losa continued to sleep. I heard Aikane's snores at the doorway.

Tears rolled down my cheeks as I realized that I'd been dreaming. Daniel wasn't there. He didn't know where I was. I rose to my knees and crawled toward the doorway.

Moonlight did indeed highlight the bay, but no tall ship approached. Thank goodness I had dreamed that too. Maybe the French wouldn't come the next day. Maybe my feet would heal in time, and I could make a run for it.

I ignored the fact that I had no idea how to get back or how to prevent the Polynesians from taking me again.

I crawled back to my mat and tentatively pressed at the soles of my feet through the bandages. Pain shot up my legs, and I gritted my teeth. No, there would be no running in the morning and maybe not the next day either, no matter where fate took me.

I lay down again and closed my eyes to dream of Daniel. I'd had no luck wishing myself back into the twenty-first century, and I wondered briefly if that was something that had occurred only on the *Vigilance*. If so, I was well and truly stuck in the past because that ship lay at the bottom of the sea. And I had no way to get back to the *Century Star*.

A few fitful hours later, the first light of dawn made its way into the hut, and I opened my eyes. I sat up to see Rimu entering the hut, as if she'd gone somewhere, and Losa stretching on her mat. She too sat up, her long glossy hair hardly needing a brush, and she rose and beckoned to me.

"Come. Aikane carry you."

"Where? I don't want to go," I said rather piteously.

"Make water," she said with her brows drawn together. "No water here?" She pointed to her lower stomach, and I understood what she was saying. Yes, I had to go to the bathroom in the worst way. I nodded.

She stepped outside and called Aikane in. As easily as Daniel had lifted me in my dream, Aikane bent and picked me up, toting me outside into the purple haze of the dewy South Pacific morning. I couldn't imagine how Aikane planned on handling me for the actual event, but I kept my mouth shut and watched as he followed Losa from her grandmother's hut and into the jungle.

I could hear the sound of running water, and we soon emerged onto a small stream that ran through the back of the village. Losa signaled that Aikane was to follow her with me in tow as she crouched unashamedly in the water.

"No, wait!" I cried out.

Aikane paused on the bank and looked down at me. I wriggled in his arms, pointlessly. Apparently Aikane had been planning to hold me in the river while I did my business. I couldn't even fathom such a thing.

Dismayed, I didn't know what to do. Not only was I disconcerted about the ecological repercussions of using the river as a toilet, I worried about disease since it seemed obvious the river was a public latrine.

"Set me down. I can manage," I said. Aikane looked over to Losa who, having seen to her needs, approached me. She spoke to him, and he set me down on the bank, following which he stepped to the edge of the river and relieved himself.

"Make water," Losa said, gesturing to the river. Aikane had turned to watch us.

"Yes, maybe, I don't know," I said. "Can you tell Aikane to turn around?"

Losa scrunched her face and shook her head, as if she didn't understand. I made a gesture for Aikane to turn away, and he didn't understand either. Then I closed my eyes and covered them with my hands in monkey-no-see fashion, and Aikane smiled. Instead of turning away, he actually covered his eyes in a surprisingly childish gesture that I found endearing.

Quickly, before Aikane opened is eyes, I hobbled to my feet, pulled up my dress and squatted in a crevice in the rock, hoping this was just a temporary solution to an urgent biological need. My feet burned mightily, but I had no time to waste. I dropped my skirts, straightened and grabbed on to Losa's arm for balance.

"Okay," I said. The view of the beautiful river nestled among tropical ferns and trees had lost its magic, and I turned away.

"Aikane," Losa called out. He dropped his hands and came to pick me up. We returned to the village just as the sun rose above the horizon. People milled about, some cooking, others visiting. Children played. I checked the bay. No large ship anchored off shore. Maybe the French wouldn't come after all. I hoped I still had time.

Aikane dropped me off, not outside to enjoy the day but inside the hut. He took up his position outside the door again. Losa wandered off, and I felt bereft without my interpreter. Rimu, preparing some foodstuffs, came over and checked on my feet. On her knees, she removed the bandages and reapplied her salve before wrapping my feet again. I had to admit that her medicine seemed to be helping, as my feet hurt just a little less than they had the day before.

"French today?" I tried asking. I hated to ask, as if I willed them to come, but I had to know.

Rimu drew her sparse gray eyebrows together and shook her head. I suspected she didn't understand my question rather than provided a negative response.

I chewed on my lip, trying to think of other ways of communicating with her. If anyone had the power to sway Kaihau, it would have been his grandmother.

"French?" I asked to see if she understood that single word.

Rimu, still on her knees, tied a final knot in my bandages and sat back. She nodded and repeated the word.

"French."

Heartened, I tried another one.

"Come?"

No, too much. She shook her head in apparent confusion.

I pointed to my chest, again nervous that I was potentially miscommunicating I wanted the French to come.

She nodded, almost warily.

"Today?"

That was the word that stumped Rimu, but I couldn't think of any other way to express the sentiment. I gave up and leaned forward to peer outside. I couldn't see the entirety of the bay but still saw no large ships.

Losa returned with Kaihau and Posoa. She carried food, which she set in the middle of the hut. Aikane joined us. I watched Kaihau carefully while we ate, but other than a glance and nod in my direction, he generally ignored me.

"Losa," I began. "Can you ask Kaihau if the French are coming today?"

She spoke to her brother, who responded.

"Say yes, today," she said.

I bit my lip. There was no point in begging anymore. And as if I had summoned the French with my incessant questions, I saw the tip of a tall mast come into view. Aikane, facing the door, saw it as well, and he said something and pointed.

Everyone with the exception of me jumped up and hurried to the door. I tried to push myself upright but lost my balance and fell down again.

"Losa!" I called out. Having followed the others outside, she didn't hear me, and I regretted speaking up. If anything, I should have avoided reminding them of my presence.

I gritted my teeth, pushed myself upright and clung to several wooden supports in the walls of the hut. I would have tried to escape out of a back door if such a thing existed, but in the absence of such, I tiptoed slowly and painfully toward the open doorway.

I stopped at the entrance and leaned heavily on the hewn log doorsill. Indeed, a large, tall three-masted ship moved slowly into the bay, and most of the villagers flocked down to the beach to await the ship's arrival. I noted that many of the females ran into the jungle.

Kaihau spoke animatedly, his excitement evident. He turned as if to enter the hut and stopped short at the sight of me. He pointed to my feet and nodded with a smile. He spoke to Losa, and she interpreted.

"Kaihau say good feet trade."

My knees weakened, and I wanted to slide down to the floor, but I stood my ground. There was no point in appearing to malinger.

Kaihau then said something to Losa, which elicited a torrent of words from Rimu and a look of shock from Losa.

The threesome exchanged a string of what sounded like angry words before Kaihau held up an imperious hand and put a stop to the discussion.

Losa turned to me.

"Aikane and Posoa take you beach. I go speak French."

"But I thought the women were going into hiding?" I said, looking at the last of them disappear into the jungle.

"Kaihau say me speak French. Grandmothers go see ship. Children go."

Kaihau spoke to Aikane and Posoa, who moved toward me. I tried to resist but they handily scooped me up into their basket hold, and away we went, heading down to the beach.

"Losa!" I called out breathlessly as she walked behind us. "Can't we talk about this? Am I going today?"

"Today," she said. "Vana home."

"Please, Losa!" I begged again. "Please ask Kaihau to give me some time."

"Please?" she repeated, seeming not to understand the rest of my words.

I wasn't sure how additional time would benefit me, but everything felt so rushed at the moment. I couldn't think straight. I shook my head, huddled in the basket and terrified of what was to come.

CHAPTER TEN

Aikane and Posoa set me down on a large black volcanic boulder on the beach. Crowds of villagers swarmed the beach, waving to the ship, seemingly harboring no grudge that the French had stolen one of their own or that the majority of their young women had to go into hiding.

I noticed that the older women and little girls had not run off to the jungle but instead held necklaces of flowers. Rimu too had followed us, but she kept a hand on Losa's arm. Aikane move to stand by Losa in a protective manner.

As I had seen with Kaihau, the village in general seemed to await the arrival of the French with an air of excitement, and I couldn't really understand why, not if the French stole women willy-nilly.

"Losa," I called above the noisy crowd. "Why is everyone so happy to see the French?"

Losa turned to me. "French good trade."

I tried to choose what few words I could use carefully. "But French take Vana? French take you?"

Her eyes rounded, and Aikane spoke to her. Her reply seemed to incense him, and his anger was directed at me. Losa stepped between him and me and said something to soothe him. Clearly he thought I was suggesting the French take her. So much for choosing my words carefully. Even Rimu glared at me.

"I didn't mean the French *should* take you, Losa."

"French no take Losa. Aikane my man," she said. Aikane grabbed Losa by the arm and angrily escorted her away from me to a spot farther down the beach. Rimu joined them, while Kaihau and Posoa remained near me.

I sighed, frustrated that I couldn't even make myself understood with such a simple question.

My stomach had knotted further every time Losa had reminded me that her brother was going to try to hand me off to the French in exchange for his lost love. I almost imagined Aikane and Posoa carrying me toward a small boat, passing Vana as she was brought to shore. Perhaps we exchanged a high five at the point of exchange, or some sort. I wouldn't even have time to ask Vana what atrocities she had experienced at the hands of the French sailors.

I shook the image from my head but shuddered when I saw the ship drop anchor, the sails lowered. About six outrigger canoes glided away from the beach carrying men toward the ship.

With all eyes on the French vessel, I scanned the area behind me—the village, the mountains behind it. I saw no way that I could escape, not really. All I could do was turn my attention forward and watch the canoes cleave through the turquoise lagoon.

Even from this distance, I could see men moving about on the ship but I couldn't make out any specific details. As soon as the canoes reached the ship, men climbed down rope ladders to jump into the small boats.

I began to shake. Oddly, though the Polynesians had kidnapped me, I feared the French more.

The canoes swung away from the ship and headed back to shore, carrying fully clothed men, distinct from the half-clad Polynesians. My trembling increased with every stroke of the oars. As the canoes headed straight for us, I threw another desperate glance over my shoulder in a futile search for escape. But it was too late. I turned around to watch in terror as the lead canoe beached directly in front of us.

The villagers pulled the boat onshore, and Kaihau moved forward to hail the five sailors descending from the boat. I don't know if I'd been expecting pegged-legged pirates, but the dark-blue uniform jackets suggested they belonged to a navy, probably the French Navy. Most of the men wore loose-fitting white trousers and shirts suitable for the tropical climate. Most covered their heads with flat-brimmed boaters.

Speaking with Kaihau was a man of obvious authority, dressed far more meticulously than the sailors, in a trim royal-blue jacket and trousers. He removed his bicorn hat, revealing well-manicured dark curls and long sideburns. He carried a sword at his side, and like the other sailors, he sported a pistol thrust into a leather belt at his waist. At his side was another much taller man with light-brown hair and a mustache, who also appeared to be an officer.

If I had wondered before how the Polynesians and French communicated, I realized then that Kaihau had a passing command of French. As villagers crowded around the sailors with leis of flowers and leaves, Kaihau spoke to the leader of the French sailors, gesticulating wildly and often pointing to me.

The dark-haired officer studied me as Kaihau talked. When the group moved toward me, I cringed.

Unexpectedly bright-blue eyes regarded me as the Frenchman stopped in front of me.

He said something over his shoulder, and most of his men melted away into the crowd of welcoming villagers. I wondered for the tenth time how they could welcome someone who had kidnapped one of their women.

A brief courtly bow took me by surprise.

"*Madame*," the Frenchman began in a cultured accent. "Please allow me to introduce myself. I am Captain Jean-Louis Sebastian, and this is my first officer, Lieutenant Francois Gappard. My friend Kaihau tells me your name is 'Mah-gee'?"

"Maggie Wollam," I managed to squeak out through dry lips. "Look. I don't know what Kaihau told you, but he kidnapped me, and I'm not available for trade! No!"

I wanted to tell him that I had friends who would come for me, but that wasn't true. And if it were, it would only put them in danger.

Captain Sebastian blinked.

"You are American, *madame*?"

I nodded. He turned to speak to Kaihau, but I couldn't make out any words. They spoke at length, Kaihau very animated, the captain noncommittal. Lieutenant Gappard watched the proceedings intently.

Captain Sebastian returned his attention to me again.

"I see," he said. "Kaihau is misinformed about Vana. I say this to you in English, given that he does not understand. We did not *take* his woman. Vana asked to come with us. She fell in love with my second mate, Charles, and she has gone to live on another island where he has a house."

Kaihau looked at us hopefully.

"Why didn't you tell him?" I asked.

"These matters of the heart are very delicate." He cast a sideways glance at Kaihau. "And I am not prepared to engage in a war with

Kaihau over a woman. You see happiness and gaiety around you as they greet us, but do not for one moment, *madame*, believe that they will not attack us and slit our throats or rip out our entrails if they believe they have been wronged."

Despite the warm sunshine, a cold shiver ran down my back.

"And you? How came you to be on this island? From where did Kaihau kidnap you?"

"We were shipwrecked."

"And who is we?"

I hesitated. I had no idea what the status of the French and Americans was in 1847. I didn't think we'd been at war, but I couldn't remember my history, and at the moment, I was too panicked to think straight.

If not, if Captain Sebastian was as reasonable as he appeared, could he sail around the island to rescue Daniel and the others?

I simply couldn't think things through at the moment.

Kaihau, growing impatient, interrupted in a spatter of French. Captain Sebastian responded to him slowly, as if he sought the right words. Even in a foreign language, I could tell he was stalling. I heard Vana's name mentioned.

The captain turned to me.

"No matter, I think I must send you to the ship at once, *Madame* Wollam, for your safety. We have some business to conduct here on the island and do not set sail until the morning, but I fear Kaihau grows angry that I am not able to produce Vana today. Lieutenant Gappard will accompany you to the ship."

I opened my mouth to protest. Captain Sebastian had seemed so reasonable. Couldn't he just let me go?

"Kaihau angry?" Losa asked me. I hadn't noticed Losa and Aikane approach from behind. Kaihau spat some words out at her and pointed to the captain. The situation seemed to be escalating. Kaihau, normally genial, had a stubborn streak.

Captain Sebastian spoke to them in French again. In a side voice, he said to me, "I am telling them that Vana is not on the ship but on another island and that I cannot return her today."

Kaihau's voice deepened, and he developed a decidedly unpleasant snarl when he spoke.

"No Vana?" Losa asked me. I didn't dare answer her. Things were escalating, and I needed to keep my wits about me.

"Francois," Captain Sebastian said in a low voice. "Be prepared to take *Madame* Wollam aboard one of the canoes."

"What?" I whispered. "No! Wait!"

Losa looked confused, and Kaihau's eyes darkened.

"Do you wish to stay here, *madame?*" Captain Sebastian said without taking his attention off Kaihau. "As a captive?"

"I'll be a captive on your ship, Captain, unless you're agreeing to—" I stopped short. *Return me to the other side of the island? Pick Daniel and the others up? And do what with them?*

"Are you at war with the Americans or anything?"

"I beg pardon?" Captain Sebastian looked as if he barely heard me. Francois moved around to my side as if to grab me. Kaihau laid a restraining hand on my arm. Aikane and Posoa menaced, their substantially muscular chests growing visibly bigger as they inhaled deeply. Losa fretted in a combination of French and Polynesian words.

Captain Sebastian's next words to Kaihau took on a soothing tone. Kaihau calmed, albeit slowly.

"What ails your feet, *madame?*" Francois whispered to me. "Can you walk?"

"No, not very well. I cut them on coral."

Francois swept me up into his arms, and I looked over toward Kaihau. At that point I didn't know whom to trust, but screaming wasn't an option. It would only escalate matters.

Kaihau's tight face showed his anger, though he seemed bent on keeping it in check.

"No take!" Losa said, hurrying toward Francois.

Kaihau barked at her, and she stopped short, turning to throw me a concerned look.

"Mag-hee," she said, holding up a hand in farewell.

Francois moved away with me toward the outrigger canoe, and at a word from Kaihau, several Polynesians jumped into the boat. I looked over Francois's shoulder to see Captain Sebastian speaking to the group, his hands raised as if to calm them.

Francois deposited me onto a bench in the canoe and jumped in behind me. The Polynesians pushed off, and the boat glided out into the lagoon. I looked back toward shore. Captain Sebastian, still alive and on both feet, moved with Kaihau and the group toward the village. Unaware of the tension surrounding the meeting, the rest of the Polynesians sang and danced. I saw myriad puffs of smoke throughout the village from what I assumed were roasting pits. It appeared as if a feast was about to get underway...for everyone except the young women hiding in the jungle.

The ship, a massive wooden hulk with three tall masts supporting furled sails, loomed larger as we approached. I threw a longing look over my shoulder again. I didn't want to leave the island, didn't want to leave Daniel behind. But freedom of choice was something I hadn't enjoyed in quite some time.

The canoe came up alongside the massive dark timbers on the hull of the ship. I looked up several stories to see an ominous row of cannons that stretched from stern to bow.

"If you please, *madame*," Francois said, standing to take my hand. I gasped as he hoisted me over his shoulder like a child on a piggyback ride.

"Hold tightly," he advised as he climbed up a ladder rope. To say that I felt foolish wrapping my legs around the waist of a strange man didn't do justice to the surreal moment.

I marveled at Francois's strength as he handily hauled both of us up the steep sides of the ship. Several sailors on deck awaited us, and Francois dropped me in the surprised arms of a foul-smelling, burly red-bearded middle-aged French sailor.

"*Madame*," the sparsely toothed man said in a form of greeting.

"Hello," I said, loosely wrapping my arms around his thick neck.

Francois said something to the redhead, and he followed Francois across the deck and toward a door. I would have stuck my feet out to block our entry if I could, but at the last minute, I remembered why I was being carried. My feet would not have welcome being used so forcefully.

"Red" carried me through the door, huffing and puffing. Probably twenty years older than Francois and a great deal heavier, he struggled under my weight.

"I can try to walk," I said.

He scrunched his forehead and shook his head.

"Do you speak English?"

"Red" apparently spoke just enough English to shake his head again.

"*Non*," he said. "*Je ne parle pas anglais.*"

Francois paused before a door and opened it, allowing "Red" to carry me through into a cabin not much larger than a walk-in closet.

"I am sorry, *madame*. The captain and I are the only ones who speak English. Jacques will see to your needs. I must return to shore."

As Jacques set me down onto a small trundle bunk attached to a wall, Francois spoke to him, gave me a short salute and left the cabin.

I eyed my burly redheaded captor/caretaker as he leaned over a small dresser and checked the contents of a pewter pitcher near a bowl of the same material.

He turned and rattled off some words in French. I think I understood the word for water. He made a universal gesture of hand to mouth and lifted his bushy eyebrows, as if asking about food. I shrugged. Hunger was the last thing on my mind. Jumping off the boat appealed to me more.

Jacques returned my shrug and left the cabin. I heard the door lock behind him, but that didn't deter me from climbing off the bed and crawling over to the door to pull at the lever. Locked. No way out. So, I was a prisoner after all, no matter how nice Captain Sebastian had seemed.

I crawled back to the bed, hoisted myself up and settled back down on top of the gray blanket, listening to the occasional creaking of timber as the ship bobbed in calm waters. I heard occasional random shouts by men on deck, but nothing in their tone suggested alarm. All seemed peaceful, except the tumult in my heart and brain.

I worried that I might never see Daniel again. Unless I told Captain Sebastian about the others, how would it be possible? But I was locked in a cabin on board the French naval vessel. If I'd had any trust for the captain at all, I had lost that when they locked me in, perhaps when Francois had manhandled me onto the ship.

So no, I wasn't inclined to tell the French about my group of fellow castaways. But if I couldn't see Daniel again, I prayed I would be able to return to the twenty-first century.

Jacques returned in a few minutes with a wooden bowl of some kind of broth and a slab of brown bread. I took them from him gingerly, fairly sure I had no intention of eating either. Food on a nineteenth-century ship and food on a tropical island seemed worlds apart in terms of health consequences.

"When is Captain Sebastian coming back to the ship?" I asked.

Jacques tilted his head.

"*Captain Sebastian?*" he repeated.

"*Oui!*" I nodded, daring to use a random word of French. "When is he coming back?"

I couldn't understand Jacques's response, and the vigorous shake of his head showed he didn't understand me. I sighed heavily and gave him a faint nod.

Jacques left, locking the door behind him. I sniffed the soup, but the pungent odor and odd bits of unidentifiable items floating around discouraged me from even trying it. The bread, hard as a rock, worried me. I had no dental coverage in the nineteenth century. I bent over and set the food down on the floor.

Straightening, I pulled my legs up onto the bunk, pulled them to my chest and laid my head down on a foul-smelling hard pillow. Closing my eyes, I wished and hoped and prayed that I would open them to find myself anywhere but on the French ship...anywhere else at all.

I must have fallen asleep.

CHAPTER ELEVEN

Even before I opened my eyes, I recognized a familiar smell of generic bleached cloth, felt the smooth feel of cotton near my cheek.

I inhaled deeply and forced open my eyelids to see sunlight peeping in through a crack in the curtains leading to the balcony. The balcony?

With a gasp, I pushed myself upright. The *Century Star*! I had traveled through time again!

I jumped off the bed, staggering as searing pain ripped through my feet. Grabbing on to a chair, I leaned against it as the pain receded, then lifted up on my toes and limped across the cabin toward the curtains. Pulling them aside, I saw not a small island but a sparkling blue sea.

I turned and surveyed the cabin. Everything was in place. My luggage rested in a corner, a bottle of water sat on the nightstand by the bed, a sheet of paper—no doubt the ship's daily activities—lay on the floor by the door, as if it had been slipped in.

I pulled open the balcony door and stepped out, dropping onto one of the two deck chairs.

I was back! I had fallen asleep on the French ship and traveled back in time. I doubted that my wishing, hoping and praying had been the catalyst. It seemed likely that I traveled through time while on board a ship—a French ship, the *Century Star* or the *Vigilance*. But the *Vigilance* was gone. I had no way to get back to Daniel.

My throat closed over, and a dull ache seized my chest. Daniel's face swam before me as I fought against tears. I fought to put his image from my mind for the moment. I didn't know what to do, but I had to do something.

My stomach rumbled distressfully, and I realized it had been hours since I'd eaten. I had no idea how long I had slept—time seemed like such a surreal concept at the moment.

I pushed myself out of the chair, clung to the door and worked my way into the bathroom by hanging on to the furniture. I stripped off my soiled and tattered dress and pulled the bandages from my feet, and after turning on the water and gathering my soaps, I lowered myself to the shower floor and sat there sobbing while I washed the sea salt and sweat from my body.

Following an extended shower, I dried off, applied antibiotic ointment to my feet and did my best to cover the cuts and scrapes with the small adhesive strips I'd brought with me. Hardly adequate coverings. I briefly thought about a visit to the ship's doctor but decided against it. I wasn't sure if the ship had stopped at a port while I'd been gone—or even sure how long I had been gone—and I didn't want to incite any curiosity about cuts from coral. A check of my wounds showed no spreading redness, and I thought I was probably safe from infection.

I contemplated the long painful trip to the nearest restaurant and opted to call room service. After throwing on the ship-provided white cotton robe and wrapping a towel around my wet hair, I climbed back onto the bed, checked the menu and dialed for food.

While I waited for a sandwich made with fresh bread and properly refrigerated ingredients, I drank the entire bottle of filtered water. Still parched, I eagerly anticipated the pitcher of iced water I had ordered with my meal.

I eyed my purse on the desktop and reached for it. Dragging my phone out, I studied the face. Two days had passed since I'd left—the hour was 2:00 p.m. I wondered what my cabin steward had thought when he saw my bed unmade for two days. When would a cabin attendant raise a "missing passenger" or "passenger overboard" alarm?

I shrugged and checked my phone once again. My original purpose in dragging it out was to check the Internet. I hadn't originally purchased onboard Internet coverage because I felt I didn't need it. But now I needed to find Daniel in time. I needed to see if there was a reference to him somewhere on the Internet.

As I attempted to negotiate the ship's website to purchase an Internet plan, I heard a knock on the door and heard a voice call out "room service."

"Come in," I said.

A petite young woman pushing a metal cart entered the room.

"Good afternoon, madam," she said, dark hair gleaming in a tight bun at the back of her head.

"Oh, hello!" I said, pathetically grateful to see and speak to someone in the twenty-first century.

"Thank you!" I said as she set down an appealing plate, holding a sandwich and fries, on the desktop, along with a pitcher of ice water and a clean drinking glass.

"You are welcome, madam," she said, her English sweetly accented. "Will there be anything else?"

I reached into my purse for a tip and handed it to her.

"No, thank you. Wait, yes!" Loath to let her go, I called her back as she turned to push the cart away.

"Yes, madam?"

"I...uh...I..."

She waited patiently.

"Where are we?"

"Madam? In your cabin?" She looked down at the room service ticket as if searching for a cabin number.

"No, I mean...where is the ship?"

"Ah!" She nodded. "I am not sure. We reach Tahiti tomorrow, I believe? Perhaps the next day. I am not sure."

"Oh!" I had forgotten the itinerary. My original trip aboard the *Century Star* seemed so remote, as if years had passed since I'd boarded the ship. In some ways, they had.

"Thank you," I said, still reluctant to let her go but unable to delay her departure any longer. It wasn't as if I could ask her to sit down with me while I ate. I couldn't very well share my adventures of the past few days. I couldn't tell her about Daniel.

"Good afternoon, madam," the room service attendant said as she left the room.

"Bye."

I picked up my sandwich and devoured it. Fresh, delicious and most likely untainted, I savored the flavors long after the food hit my stomach. I munched on potato chips and eyed my phone again, opting to wait until I wiped my hands before handling the phone.

I finished my meal, picked up the phone and stretched back against the soft pillows, luxuriating in the comfort of the bed and cleanliness of the room and my body.

After some finagling, I managed to sign up for the Internet. The speed of connection was dauntingly slow, and my eyelids fluttered while I waited for a search engine to load. Satiated, warm and comfortable, my body longed for a nap. I struggled to focus on the phone screen. I straightened in the bed and widened my eyes, unwilling to fall asleep. If I fell asleep, I might possibly travel through time again. But to where?

I pinched myself a couple of times and drank ice-cold water to help stay awake.

Refocusing on my phone again, I keyed in "Dr. Daniel Hawthorne," which brought up multiple results. All appeared to be current references to physicians in California, New York and Massachusetts. Nothing seemed remotely historical.

The ship! The *Vigilance*. Surely if it sank, there would be a historical article describing the event...and perhaps the fate of the crew.

I keyed in *"Vigilance"* and came up with a World War II minesweeper commissioned in 1944. No matter how many different ways I spelled *"Vigilance,"* I could find no references to a nineteenth-century merchant ship sailing out of San Francisco.

My eyelids drooped as I fruitlessly scanned my phone. My head bobbed, and I straightened once again. Another sip of ice water did nothing to awaken me. I thought about getting up and walking around the room, but my feet begged me to stay put.

Try as I might, I couldn't fight the heavy lethargy that hit me, and I leaned my head back on the pillow.

Within what seemed like a matter of moments—I was soon to discover hours—I heard the unmistakable sounds of timber creaking. The smell of salt and pitch brought me fully awake, and I bolted upright.

Through a faint light in a porthole, the tiny shoebox cabin on the French ship materialized before me. I had fallen asleep and traveled back in time. The insanity of the travel was truly driving me crazy.

I jumped off the trundle bed, pain searing through my feet. Looking down, I noted with shock that I still wore the ship's cotton bathrobe. I pulled it tightly around me, wondering how I was going to explain my change of clothes to Jacques, to Captain Sebastian.

I limped over to the porthole. Dusk had descended in the South Pacific, and I realized I must have slept for hours—whether in the twenty-first century or the nineteenth century, it hardly seemed to matter.

A faint scratching sound caught my ear, and I whirled around. There on the floor was the bowl of broth and bread that Jacques had brought me. And feasting on the bread was a small rat.

With a screech, I jumped up onto a small wooden chair. Crouching hurt my feet, so I stood upright, my head almost touching the ceiling. A sound at the door both startled and relieved me. Jacques could get rid of the rodent. I wondered if I would be able to sleep that night. Surely that wasn't the only rat on the ship.

The door opened quietly, and a shadowy figure stepped in.

"Jacques! Help me! A rat!" I pointed.

I should have realized from the man's height that it wasn't Jacques.

"Hush, Maggie. It is I, Daniel." He moved toward me and pulled me from the chair to cradle me in his arms.

"Daniel!" I whispered, wrapping my arms around his neck. "Oh, Daniel! How did you find me? How did you know?"

"Frederick, apparently unable to sleep, saw you taken. Rather than delay to awaken us and effect a rescue, he followed your captors, then returned to us the following morning to apprise us of your kidnapping."

Daniel pulled me closer to him.

"I will tell you the rest later. We must leave. What is this that you are now clothed in?"

"I traveled forward in time to the *Century Star*. It's a cotton bathrobe. I didn't know I was going to travel back again, or I would have changed."

Daniel turned for the door.

"So you *can* still travel through time?"

"Yes, apparently if I'm on a ship. At least that's what I think. You can put me down, Daniel. I can try to keep up."

"Are your feet miraculously healed by the time travel?" he murmured.

"No, not quite."

"Then I will carry you." With one hand, he pulled open the door.

"How did you get the key? Where is Jacques? The captain?"

"Later," Daniel whispered. He carried me up onto the deck, which was surprisingly quiet. A glance toward shore showed bonfires burning in the growing darkness. I saw people moving in the village, heard singing and laughter. It seemed as if any visit from the French was a cause for celebration, unless they stole one of the young women.

The silence aboard the ship suggested that almost everyone was onshore. Where was Jacques? I wanted to ask Daniel again but bit my lip.

Daniel carried me to the railing and set me down on my feet. I balanced on my toes precariously while I watched him climb over the railing to step onto a rope ladder. He reached for me, and I maneuvered myself over the railing, where Daniel tucked me between his chest and the ladder. We descended the ladder slowly, the rope rungs tearing at the soles of my feet.

An outrigger canoe awaited us at the waterline, where Frederick took hold of me without a word and settled me onto a bench.

"Where did you get this?" I whispered to Daniel, who followed me and took up an oar.

"We stole it," Daniel said. "Off we go, boys."

Frederick thrust an oar against the hull of the ship and pushed away. Samuel, whom I had just noticed, stuck an oar into the water and paddled quietly. Daniel joined them with a third oar. We moved away from the ship and, to my surprise, out to sea.

"Where are we going?"

"Back to our encampment. We have to move away from shore so that we are undetected," Daniel said. "Following that, I am not certain. We could attempt to move further inland to hide from the Polynesians if the ladies can make that journey. This canoe is too small for all of us to venture out to sea to find another island, and even if we could find another place, there may be more Polynesians who think nothing of kidnapping women. Why did they take you? Why did they hand you over to the French? We watched the exchange from the cliff above the village but could not hear."

"The chief, a young man named Kaihau, took me to exchange for his girlfriend—or fiancée—whom he thought had been taken by the French. Little does Kaihau know that Vana left voluntarily with a French sailor and is now living on a nearby island. I'm not sure how Captain Sebastian was going to deal with that. I think the captain thought he was rescuing me. I'm not sure what he planned to do with me, but he seemed a decent enough sort of man. Except I was locked in the cabin, so clearly I couldn't leave if I wanted. I dared not tell anyone about the rest of you though."

"Captain Sebastian?" Daniel repeated. "I have heard of him. You are well away from him. I have heard he does not like to be thwarted."

"Really? He seemed very pleasant actually."

"Pleasant?" Daniel said in a gruff voice. He looked over his shoulder toward me.

"Did he release you? Were you not restrained in a locked cabin?" He turned to face forward.

"Well, yes. But he took me back to the ship to get me out of Kaihau's hands."

Daniel spoke over his shoulder. "Yes, this story of the chief, Kaihau, and his woman, Vana. You have only Captain Sebastian's word that she left voluntarily. In my experience, these women do not leave their families. The husband is expected to join *her* family."

"Oh!" I said. "I believed him. He seemed so—"

"Honorable?" Daniel asked.

"I guess," I murmured.

"Nonetheless, we have you back now. It is possible that Captain Sebastian may come for you. Or he may not. I do not know. I had to incapacitate a rather rotund redheaded fellow to effect your rescue. Is that the Jacques you asked about?"

I nodded.

"This man, Jacques, saw me, so Captain Sebastian may seek revenge or—"

"I didn't tell him about you. He wondered if I was alone, but I didn't tell him about the group."

"He will know that you were not alone before long."

"I just can't imagine Captain Sebastian pursuing us," I murmured.

"And if he does not, it is possible the Polynesians will return for the rest of us."

"Why?"

"To kill us, I presume," he said in a grim voice.

"No!" I sputtered. "No, they wouldn't. They seem so peaceful, so friendly, with the exception of taking me."

"I do not know these particular islanders, Maggie, but I can assure you that Polynesians have killed intruders to protect their homes and their islands. They have been vastly put upon over the years—kidnapped, enslaved, used abominably, even murdered. I am pleased that they treated you well during your time with them, but do not imagine them as pacifists."

I fell silent and turned to watch the village bonfires, now fading in the distance as the canoe moved beyond the bay. A bright moon shone down on us, allowing the men to see the coastline to navigate around the island.

I crawled over to sit beside Daniel as he rowed.

"Daniel," I began in a low voice. "If we can't run, then we have to figure out how to negotiate with Kaihau and his people."

"How? We have no assurance that they won't kill us, Maggie. How did you even manage to communicate with them? Do they speak English?"

"Kaihau's sister, Losa, speaks English. I think she learned from a missionary."

"Do you mean to say there is an English missionary in the village? That is a hopeful sign."

"No, not that I saw. But I could try to talk to Kaihau through Losa, to explain that we're trapped here on the island—" Then I thought of the French naval ship.

"Wait, Daniel! Are we really trapped? Couldn't we have hitched a ride with the French to Tahiti or a more populated island?"

"I would not think the captain would be inclined to do anything for us as a group at this point, since I assaulted his man and spirited you away. He will probably not take kindly to your disappearance. Whether he chooses to pursue us or not is anyone's guess. We should prepare for such. But to answer your question, no, I do not believe we can ask Captain Sebastian for safe passage."

I lowered my voice and leaned near Daniel.

"Not to mention I would probably travel forward in time again if I fall sleep on the ship."

"Under the present circumstances, Maggie, that would be a blessing for you. If I thought you safe, I would return you to the ship at once. Given your belief that you only travel through time on ships, I was surprised that I was able to find you on the French vessel. Surprised though pleased."

I nodded.

"I know! Your timing was perfect. I had *just* returned."

Daniel gave me a sideways glance. "Ah, yes. The robe. What shall we do with that?"

"I have no idea."

"I suspect the ladies will have something to say about your attire."

"Yes, I'm sure they will. I'll just tell them the French made me wear it."

He glanced at me again.

"I am not certain they will have seen such material, but perhaps they will not notice."

"Terry cloth," I said, fingering the sash of the robe. "It's terry cloth. Like towels."

"Not like any towels that I have ever seen."

"No, probably not," I acknowledged.

Daniel pulled on his oar and chuckled.

"It is peculiar that we find ourselves speaking of cloth."

"Everything about this is peculiar."

"Yes, indeed."

Daniel fell silent, and I turned to look over my shoulder. I could see neither the village nor the French ship any longer. We must have rounded the island.

"Steady now, boys! We do not want to be dragged into the coral reef. Pull hard and row for the break," Daniel called out. I turned to look to the right. White waves, visible under the moonlight, crashed against the reef. I felt the canoe accelerate as waves pushed it toward the reef.

"Pull!" Daniel yelled. "Keep the canoe steady!"

"We're trying, Doctor!" one of them yelled back.

"Hang on, Maggie! Take hold of me and hang on!" Daniel shouted.

I bit my lip and wrapped my arms around Daniel's waist as the canoe lifted up on a wave and crashed down.

CHAPTER TWELVE

But we didn't hit the reef. The men managed to keep the canoe from crashing into the destructive coral until they found the cut in the reef. They maneuvered the boat through the break and then glided on into the peaceful lagoon.

I saw a figure running on the beach. Small and energetic, it looked like Thomas. We rowed toward shore, and he ran into the water to help pull the canoe onto the sand.

"Where are the ladies?" Daniel asked him.

"Sleeping," he said. "Where did you get this boat?" he asked with rounded eyes.

"We stole it," Daniel said.

"Mrs. Wollam! Welcome back! What happened?"

"We will tell you later, Thomas," Daniel said. "Right now I think we could all use something to drink and a bit of food. There is a possibility that we may be pursued, and we might not have much time to move, but move away from our present location we must. We are too exposed here."

Daniel picked me up in his arms and stepped onto the sand. He carried me toward the A-line huts just inside the tree line. At the sound of our arrival, Mrs. Darymple stepped outside of her hut. She saw me and rushed forward as Daniel lowered me to the sand in front of my hut. She knelt down next to me and grabbed my hand.

"Maggie, my dear! You are safely back. Wherever did you go?" I noted that she eyed my robe but said nothing.

"We do not have much time, Mrs. Darymple," Daniel said. "Mrs. Wollam was kidnapped by islanders intent on trading her to the French for a convoluted purpose. We rescued her from a French naval vessel, but I had to overcome one of their sailors to do so. I expect that we will soon be pursued by the islanders or the French or perhaps both, possibly as early as dawn. We must leave the encampment, but as to where, I am not yet certain."

"Islanders? Do you mean Polynesians?"

"Yes."

"Then we are not alone on the island."

"No," I said. "There's a large village further along the coast."

"And you were kidnapped and traded to the French? How very extraordinary! And what did the French intend to do with her?" She looked up at Daniel.

"Well, I think the captain wanted to rescue me from the Polynesians."

"Though I found her on board the French vessel, locked in a cabin," Daniel growled.

"Locked in a cabin? Oh, that sounds ominous," Mrs. Darymple said. She scanned my robe once again, and I tugged at each side to pull it closer.

At the movement, she patted my hand. "There, there, my dear. No need to worry about that now. Dr. Hawthorne has rescued you, and that is that."

"Yes, but we need to strategize," Daniel said. "We can do one of three things. Take the canoe out to sea and attempt to search for another island, but we do not know if any islands are nearby, nor do I know if the canoe could hold all of us. Then, how could we provision it for a journey of what might be several days or more?

"We could take the canoe around toward the east side of the island to search for another beach, but it is likely the islanders might also sail the perimeter of the island to search for us. Likely the French might do so as well.

"Our final and, I think, best option is to move inland. We could scuttle the canoe by overturning it and pushing it out of the lagoon to suggest that we drowned in a mishap. We could then move inland until we determine that the islanders and the French no longer pursue us. We can always send one or two of the boys to fish or collect seafood with which to supplement our diet."

"I agree with you," I said. "Moving inland would be best."

"Is there is no chance that we can negotiate with the French?" Mrs. Darymple asked. "For passage off the island? I do have money."

"No, I do not think so, Mrs. Darymple. As I mentioned, I struck one of their sailors, rendering him insensible. Further, I fear this Captain Sebastian will attempt to retake Mrs. Wollam."

"Why should they retake her?" Mrs. Darymple asked.

"The French captain has a reputation. I do not wish to say more." Daniel looked away.

"Then let us not delay," Mrs. Darymple said, as if understanding Daniel's cryptic remark. "I shall waken Agatha at once, though how she has slept through our noise is beyond my comprehension."

Mrs. Darymple rose slowly and stepped into her hut.

"Come, boys," Daniel said. "Let us dispose of the canoe. Frederick, please stay with the women for their safety."

"Yes, sir," he said.

"I hate to see our only way off the island pushed out to sea," I said softly.

"I understand," Daniel said. "And yet I cannot imagine floating about the ocean in such a small vessel."

"Yes, I agree."

The men, including Thomas, moved away, and I watched as they pushed the canoe into the lagoon. They jumped in and rowed away toward the break in the reef. Frederick sat down beside me to join me in my vigil. I sensed he wished he could have gone with them.

"It is the middle of the night, Mrs. Darymple. Surely this can wait until morning? I can barely see in the dark." I heard Mrs. Simpson fussing. Frederick and I turned to see the women emerging from the hut.

"No, Agatha. I think urgency is of the utmost."

"But what is happening?"

"Here is Mrs. Wollam back. She was kidnapped by Polynesians and the French, and it is likely that one or the other are coming back here."

"What? Kidnapped? The French? Are there other people on the island then? Are we to be rescued?"

"No, Agatha. I am afraid I do not have time to explain all. Slip your boots on, there's a good girl. We have to flee."

"I do not understand," Mrs. Simpson fretted. She sat down on the sand near me and laced up her boots in the dark.

"Mrs. Wollam, we wondered what had become of you," she said. "I do not understand. Here is one young man, but where are the rest of the men, Mrs. Darymple?" She looked up as Mrs. Darymple lowered herself and sat down next to her.

"They have gone to overturn the canoe and will return shortly."

"Canoe? What is a canoe? I see a moving shape in the water. Is that a small boat?" She peered out onto the lagoon, the translucent color well lit under moonlight.

"Yes, Agatha, that is Dr. Hawthorne, the men and Thomas. They are in a canoe, a Polynesian boat."

"But where are they going?"

"I told you. To overturn it, to scuttle it. It seems we may be in danger from the Polynesians, perhaps the French. At the very least, one or the other will come in search of us. Dr. Hawthorne feels that if we overturn the canoe and send it out to sea, our pursuers will think we sailed out and were all drowned."

"But a perfectly good boat!"

"Yes, I feel the same way. Nevertheless, we would not know where to go, where the next island might be. Dr. Hawthorne feels we must move inland and hide."

"Inland?" Mrs. Simpson looked over her shoulder toward the darkness of the tree line behind us.

"Don't worry, Mrs. Simpson," I spoke up. "I think we'll be safer inland than at sea. Hopefully, they won't come looking for us at all, but in case they do, we can hide in the jungle."

"Jungle? Jungle?" Mrs. Simpson fretted again.

I shared her fears but kept them to myself. The thick foliage behind us swayed and rustled ominously in the night breezes, and I didn't know how we could find our way in the darkness. I had seen some of the jungle and even reveled in its beauty, but we could not go in that direction. We were about to embark on a journey at night through thick jungle with two elderly women and a cripple.

I rose to stand, determined not to be a burden. Frederick jumped up though to help steady me. My feet burned with the weight, but slightly less than they had the day before. Surely with some sort of stick as a cane, I could make my own way to wherever we chose to go.

"Are you in pain, madam?"

"A little," I murmured. "But I have to get up one way or the other if we're to travel."

"I do not understand," Mrs. Simpson continued. "Why would the French pursue us? We have no quarrel with them."

"It is not clear that they will, Agatha. We have no way of knowing. Please try not to worry. We are together, we are alive, and we have four big strong men to care for us."

I turned to look at the lagoon. Four ghostly silhouettes moved toward us. I knew it was the men and Thomas wading through the shallow water on their return, but the sight terrified me. The hair on my scalp rose. I resisted an urge to drop down and bury myself in the sand like a turtle. Gritting my teeth, I watched.

Ten minutes later, the men emerged onto the beach, recognizable as Daniel, Samuel, James and young Thomas.

Soaking wet, all of them, I worried that they had no spare dry clothing. The night air was balmy, but I saw slender Thomas shivering. I wrapped an arm around him. He froze in my embrace, and I gave up nurturing him and dropped my arms. He flashed me a faint smile and returned to shivering like the other men.

"Come. We must go. Did you explain all to Mrs. Simpson?" Daniel asked us.

"As best that I could," Mrs. Darymple said.

"Maggie, I see that you are standing bravely, but I think I must carry you."

"No, you can't possibly carry me all the way through the jungle. I can walk. Maybe if I lean on someone?"

"Yes, of course," Daniel said, slipping a supporting arm around my waist. My heart fluttered, as it always did with his touch.

"Fortunately, we have a measure of moonlight with which to find our way," Daniel said. "We will head away from the village."

Frederick helped Mrs. Simpson to her feet, and Samuel took charge of Mrs. Darymple.

Daniel led the way slowly past the huts, half carrying me despite my best intentions. I really couldn't walk very well. We stepped into the tree line and moved between trees. We picked our way through the thick foliage for a while until a path of some sort presented itself.

"This can't be good," I whispered, not wanting the others to hear.

"The trail is narrow, likely used by animals, perhaps a boar. I have seen them on the Polynesian islands before."

"A boar?" I squeaked.

"Perhaps," Daniel said.

I strained to see if some hairy little creature with gleaming eyes and sharp tusks awaited us on the path, but could see little now that the overhead canopy of trees blocked much of the moon.

"Do they attack?"

"They could, I imagine. Still, better to face a boar than your newfound friends."

"Which? The Polynesians or the French?" I asked, peering into the darkness again for any sign of movement. "I still don't feel like either group was going to harm me."

"It is difficult to know. The Polynesians were certainly prepared to trade you to a ship full of men, and the French more than happy to incarcerate you." Daniel's voice deepened, and he pulled me closer to him. At the moment, I didn't care what surrounded us. I felt utterly safe in his arms.

"Doctor, I recognize this path. I know where we are," Samuel said from behind us. "This is the way to the pool where we found the water."

Daniel stopped and turned.

"To the pool? Do you think it safe there?"

"It seemed very secluded," James offered.

"Then that is where we will go...for now," Daniel said. "Lead the way, gentlemen."

Samuel moved ahead with Mrs. Darymple. James and Thomas followed them, while Frederick lagged behind us with a sagging Mrs. Simpson.

We traveled on for another half hour or so until the sound of rushing water caught our ears. I noted that the sky had lightened to a soft charcoal gray, as if dawn approached.

We came upon a small opening in the jungle and stopped just as the trees fell away to reveal the source of the water. A delightful waterfall cascaded down into a pool of water. I imagined that must be what paradise looked like. In muted predawn shades of purple, blue and green, the tropical oasis beckoned.

The others reached us, and together we gazed upon the scene. When James and Thomas stepped forward, Daniel stalled them.

"Wait! You will be quite exposed if you step out into the open. Let us pause here temporarily in the sanctuary of the trees, perhaps allow the ladies to rest."

"This would be a lovely place to relocate," Mrs. Darymple said.

"Yes, I agree," Daniel said. "And yet I fear the Polynesians must know about the existence of this oasis. The island is not immense."

"I cannot go on," Mrs. Simpson said. "I cannot. Can I sit?"

"Yes, of course, Mrs. Simpson." Frederick settled her onto a fallen tree.

Daniel eyed her and sighed heavily.

"Yes, the women must rest. If we see nothing or anyone worrisome, we might be able to establish a temporary camp here." Daniel lowered me to the tree next to Mrs. Simpson, and Samuel did the same with Mrs. Darymple.

"We will reconnoiter the area to see if there have been signs of human habitation or use," Daniel said. "We shall not go far."

The men and Thomas moved out, Daniel pointing toward the perimeter of the oasis. Through the trees, I could see Daniel and Thomas carefully pick their way through the foliage to the right, while the other three men circled the oasis to the left. I lost sight of them within minutes.

"Did I hear the doctor mention wild animals? A boar? What is a boar?" Mrs. Simpson asked, her voice higher than normal.

"A wild hairy pig, Agatha," Mrs. Darymple said. "I have read about them. Yes, I would imagine there might be wild animals in the jungle."

"Oh no," Mrs. Simpson moaned.

I sympathized with her and scanned our surroundings with unease. The men returned in about ten minutes and rallied for a discussion.

"There are no signs of use—no evidence of campfires, no human debris. I think we might do well here for a while." Daniel smiled encouragingly. "If you ladies are in agreement, I think the men and I will begin to build some shelters before nightfall. Perhaps you would like to go down to the water's edge to refresh yourselves, to drink some water?"

"I will help you, Maggie," Daniel said. He pulled me to my feet and led me out into the open. The sun must have risen above the horizon, and the colors in the oasis had sharpened into emerald-green ferns, a white foaming waterfall and a mirrored pool in shades of blue and black. Brilliant red, pink and yellow flowers bloomed throughout the surrounding shrubs. Ebony lava rocks reminded me once again of the island's volcanic origins.

It was on a bank of those rocks that Daniel settled me on a smooth boulder. He lowered himself to his knees and leaned into the pool, cupping his hands to gather water. My heart thumped as he brought the water to my lips. I drank from his hands, and he repeated the movement again. I could not have imagined a more romantic setting, with the exception of being alone. He watched me intently, and I almost imagined we were alone.

Daniel gathered one more handful of water, and I held his wrist ostensibly to guide the water to my mouth. I simply wanted to touch him, and I did not let go.

Birds twittered in the trees nearby. Mrs. Darymple and Mrs. Simpson, a short distance away on a small beach, drank and washed their faces. The waterfall hummed with splashing water. Sunlight filled the oasis. And Daniel leaned forward to kiss my wet lips.

CHAPTER THIRTEEN

"Dr. Hawthorne!" a female voice said reprovingly. A pulse thudded in my ears, and I wondered where the voice came from. I opened my eyes to see Daniel's dark-brown gaze watching me tenderly.

Lost in the moment, I blinked as Daniel sat back and looked over his shoulder toward the older women.

"Really, Dr. Hawthorne!" Mrs. Simpson said from where she and Mrs. Darymple sat on the beach. "Most unseemly."

"Nonsense, Agatha," Mrs. Darymple said. "Let us leave the young people alone. We must no longer be governed by such strict rules, not in our present circumstances."

My cheeks flamed, and I looked down at my lap.

With gentle fingers, Daniel lifted my chin so that I looked up at him. His bright smile held a hint of mischief.

"Do you wish to refresh yourself? Can you reach the water, or would you rather sit near the ladies?"

"No...no," I stammered. "I'm fine here. I can reach the water."

"Good. I must go help with the huts."

"Yes," I said in a dreamy voice.

He tapped my nose, then rose to move away. I watched him return to the tree line—a tall man with an easy stride. His uniform, once crisply laundered, was crumpled and crusted with sand. But he still wore it well. I imagined him lounging on one of the lava rocks in a white linen shirt and trousers, like some sort of pirate. How handsome he would look.

I turned away and lowered myself to my chest on the flat rock to cup water into my hands and wash my face. Keeping my eyes averted from the ladies, I returned to a sitting position and removed the Band-Aids from my feet with care, following which I dropped my feet into the cool water, conveniently ignoring the fact that I had also drunk water from the same pool. What was a castaway to do?

Bracing my arms behind me, I leaned back and closed my eyes, blissfully reveling in the memory of Daniel's soft kiss. A sound from behind me caught my attention, a rustling in the brush.

I popped open my eyes and twisted to search the nearby foliage. I could hear the voices of the men in the other direction but saw no one in the direction of the rustling.

I wanted to call out but dared not. If Kaihau and his men had discovered us, I didn't want to escalate the situation. Perhaps they hadn't heard the men. I threw a glance in the women's direction. By now they lay back on the beach resting. I didn't call out to them.

Just as I turned around to search the foliage again, a creature burst out of the brush and ran around the perimeter of the pool. A boar! A dark-gray hairy pig. Devoid of tusks, the little pig looked terrified as it ran away and disappeared into the brush.

I stared in the direction in which it had disappeared and raised a hand to my throat. My heart pounded, and I breathed deeply to try to slow the pace. A glance toward the still-supine Mrs. Darymple and Mrs. Simpson indicated that they had heard and seen nothing.

Shaking, I dropped down to my back and stared into the blue sky. I wanted to tell someone about the pig and hoped that I wouldn't. I didn't want the men to hunt the little thing. Having finally seen one, my fears were allayed.

Or had it been a juvenile?

I shook my head, closed my eyes and tried to relax but couldn't. Now alert to *any* noise from the brush, I fretted that Kaihau or the French might find us. And what implications that held for us. For me.

I felt more than saw a shadow blot out the warm sun, and I thrust myself up into a sitting position. Daniel stood over me, sweat pouring down his brow. He looked over his shoulder toward the women and then dropped to his knees at my side.

"Maggie, the boys and I have finished building the huts and are in desperate need of a bath. Do you think you could join the ladies in the huts so that we could bathe here in the pool? Fortunately, we found some bananas, coconuts and other tropical fruits nearby, so you could eat while we bathe."

"Sure!" I said, my face as red as Daniel's. "I'm hoping you guys will do the same for us later? I don't know about Mrs. Darymple and Mrs. Simpson, but I could use a bath as well."

"Yes, of course," he said. "In fact, the men and I should double back to the beach and see if anyone pursues us. We can gather more food along the way."

I pulled my feet from the water. They felt considerably better, as if the pool had some magical healing property, although I wasn't sure I imagined things, so beautiful was the oasis.

"I will find some more sap to soothe your feet," Daniel said, examining them. "They look better though. Are you in pain?"

"No, not when I'm sitting. They're still sore, but I'm on the mend." I smiled and put my hand in his as he helped me rise. I cinched my robe closed, wishing that I still had my flowered dress. Better yet, a pair of shorts and a T-shirt.

Daniel helped me back to the tree line where the men and Thomas had built four huts again in the same A-line configuration. The men were busily collecting palm fronds and dropping them in a pile while snacking on bananas. I suspected the ladies and I would be making mats and "blankets" again.

Daniel settled me just outside one of the huts with a pile of fruit. Frederick had worked his magic on some coconuts, leaving us with the water to drink and husks containing shredded coconut meat.

"I will just go get the ladies," Daniel said.

I nodded, hungrily peeling a banana and stuffing a few of the tart red berries in my mouth at the same time. Within minutes, Mrs. Darymple and Mrs. Simpson arrived and sat down beside me to share the food.

"So the men are to bathe," Mrs. Darymple said. "Dr. Hawthorne said that when they are done, they will return to the beach to reconnoiter and that we could bathe while they were gone."

I heard the sound of men talking and the splash of water.

"Yes, I know *I* need a bath," I said. "Though I'm not sure what I could use for soap."

"I am most certainly *not* going to disrobe around men," Mrs. Simpson said. "Not even to bathe. I will just wash my hands and face."

"As Dr. Hawthorne said, Agatha, they will leave so that we may enjoy privacy."

"No, I simply could not bathe so openly in public. I could not."

"You will soon become unbearable, Agatha, if you do not bathe."

"Additionally, I do not like the notion that the men are leaving us to fend for ourselves," Mrs. Simpson muttered. "I think they must stay here to protect us. Did we not just flee from real or imagined pursuers?"

I turned to look at the older woman, picking at her banana with a pinched expression.

"They're quite real, Mrs. Simpson, I assure you. I'm not sure either the Polynesians or the French will pursue us...me rather, but I *was* kidnapped and traded."

"I have no doubt about the veracity of your story, Mrs. Wollam," Mrs. Darymple said. "Agatha is not herself, I think."

"It all sounds so farfetched," Mrs. Simpson said in a querulous voice.

"It felt farfetched," I said, eating some coconut. I didn't take offense, but I worried about Mrs. Simpson's state of mind. She didn't seem resilient enough to handle the stresses we would likely endure for the foreseeable future. Frankly, I didn't think *I* was resilient enough.

"I do not know what would suffice for a soap, Mrs. Wollam, but I think I might try to crush the petals of some of these flowers and use the fragrance to at least scent my hair." Mrs. Darymple raised a hand to her silver hair, no longer in a tidy coif but hanging down her back.

"No, I simply cannot bathe with men nearby," Mrs. Simpson reiterated again, as if she had been arguing silently with herself. "I cannot."

"You must do as you please, Agatha," Mrs. Darymple said.

Off and on, I'd been listening to the sound of the men speaking in low tones, some masculine laughs, the splashing of water. Within a short while, a freshly washed and dazzlingly handsome Daniel appeared at the opening to the hut. He smoothed back his now curly wet dark hair and smiled.

"We will leave now. I wonder if I should leave one of the men to watch over you while we are gone. He could wait here at the huts to allow you some privacy?"

"No, certainly not!" Mrs. Simpson said.

"Now, Agatha, you said you were not going to bathe anyway."

"I actually think that would be a good idea, Daniel," I said. "I really do. If he promises not to look while we bathe?"

"Whom do you trust?" Daniel said with a broad grin, seeming somewhat happier now that he had washed off the salt water and sweat of the previous few days. I hoped we would figure out the logistics of how to wash our clothing without a spare change.

"Frederick?" Daniel offered. "He is the most sensible, I think."

"Yes, Frederick will do nicely. A very sensible boy," Mrs. Darymple said. "I have eaten enough and look forward to a nice bath." She rose.

Mrs. Simpson and I stood up as well and stepped out of the tent.

The men, waiting on Daniel, sported shinier clean faces and wet hair. They all looked happier for having bathed, and they smelled much better. Even somber Thomas grinned. From the sounds I'd heard, they had enjoyed playing in the pool.

Mrs. Darymple moved over to a bush of brilliant-pink flowers and picked a few, crushing them in her fingers. A sweet scent permeated the air, and she turned and smiled.

"Perfume for our bath," she said.

Daniel, speaking to Frederick, turned and smiled.

"Indeed. The blossom smells lovely. We will leave you now. Frederick will stay here inside one of the huts."

Daniel looked at me as if he wanted to say something but closed his mouth. He allowed his hand to brush mine before turning and leading Samuel, James and Thomas from the camp.

"I will just be inside here, ladies," Frederick said, pointing to a hut.

Mrs. Darymple and I turned to walk to the beach, and Mrs. Simpson fell in behind.

"I will not bathe, but I will await you on the beach," Mrs. Simpson said.

"Of course, Agatha," Mrs. Darymple said, slipping an arm around my waist. "Let me help you, dear."

I appreciated her support but did not lean on her overly much, given her age. For all her mental toughness, she was a frail woman, and I worried about her.

"Thank you."

We made our way to the beach, where Mrs. Simpson sat down on the sand, hunching her shoulders and turning her back to us as Mrs. Darymple and I undressed. It took me only a second to get out of my bathrobe. Mrs. Darymple required assistance unbuttoning her dress and unlacing her corset.

"Well, have you entered the water yet?" Mrs. Simpson asked in her typical querulous voice. "I have averted my eyes so long that my neck pains me."

"Agatha, for goodness' sake. You have *en dishabille* before. In fact, you have assisted me in undressing. There is no need to affect such modesty. Truly." Mrs. Darymple threw me a wry grin, and shed of her clothing, she boldly waded into the cool water.

Pale to the point of luminescence, her skin was flawless for a woman her age. She immersed herself in the pool, dunking her head and emerging from the water like a silver-haired mermaid.

Much more bashful than Mrs. Darymple, I limped as fast as I could into the water, my tender feet unoffended by the soft wet mud in the pool. Like the older woman, I dunked my head to wet my hair.

"Agatha, you really must come in. The water is absolutely delightful." Mrs. Darymple offered me a handful of the crushed paste she'd made of the flower petals.

"Thank you," I said. As I smoothed some of the paste into my hair and attempted to lather it, I noted Mrs. Simpson had turned around and regarded us with a disapproving stare. Beyond her, at the encampment, I saw no sign of Frederick. If he watched, I was happily unaware.

"Is the water cold?" Mrs. Simpson finally asked.

While the petals may not have cleaned my hair as well as I might have wished, the perfume infused the strands with a delicate sweet smell. I rubbed the rest of the paste over my body and dunked my head in the pond once again.

"Not at all, Agatha," Mrs. Darymple called out. "Come! You really would feel so much better if you were able to bathe."

"If you insist." Mrs. Simpson looked over her shoulder toward the huts and then back at us.

"Do you wish assistance with your corset?" Mrs. Darymple said. Her wet hair, streaming down over her shoulders, gleamed like a silver dollar.

"Yes, thank you."

Mrs. Darymple, again showing no signs of embarrassment, rose from the water and returned to the beach. She helped Mrs. Simpson undress. Before shedding her gown completely, Mrs. Simpson asked us to turn around. Mrs. Darymple chuckled and returned to the water, and I turned toward the waterfall. Spying a ledge just below the fall, I kicked out and swam toward it.

As I approached, the water roiled and foamed gently, and I managed to pull myself up on the smooth lava rock ledge tucked behind the waterfall. Hugging my knees to my chest, I sat under the fall and watched the cascade with delight.

I could not imagine a time in the twenty-first century when I would have sat under a tropical waterfall, naked, in the open.

"Is there room for one more?"

Mrs. Darymple reached the ledge, and I extended a hand to help her climb onto the rock.

"Agatha prefers to bathe alone," she said.

The sheet of falling water prevented us from seeing Mrs. Simpson, so she had her wish.

We sat there companionably, wet though comfortably warm, given the tropical temperatures.

"I need to wash out my things," Mrs. Darymple said. "They are infused with the scent of dried salt water."

"I'm not sure how fast they would dry," I said. "It's very humid here."

"Yes, it might take some time. I suppose I would have to hide in a hut until the clothing was sufficiently dry. Just one of many inconveniences we must face, I am afraid."

I nodded.

"I keep trying to think of ways to cope, how to manage, to improvise, but this will be a learning experience for us all. Luckily, my robe is fairly clean."

"Yes, I did notice your change of attire, but I have had no time to query you. What happened to your other gown? And what material is your robe made of?"

"Terry cloth?" Since Daniel hadn't been familiar with the term, I assumed Mrs. Darymple wasn't either. I stiffened, hoping she wouldn't ask more.

"Now tell me exactly what happened. Were you taken from your hut? How did we not hear you scream? Were you able to scream?"

"No, I had gone down to the beach to sit for a while, and I wasn't able to call out. The Polynesians covered my face in something that made me faint. Believe me—I would have screamed if I could have."

"And they took you to a village? Did they mistreat you? Other than kidnapping you, of course."

"The village is called Leakiki. And no, they didn't mistreat me. They were really very kind, solicitous of my feet. I was well taken care of by the women, one of whom spoke a little bit of English."

"Leakiki," Mrs. Darymple repeated, as if mulling the word over. "And why precisely did the Polynesians take you? How did the French become involved?"

I explained the story of Kaihau, Vana and the French. I also told Mrs. Darymple what I had learned from Captain Sebastian, that Vana had gone willingly, and that Daniel doubted such a story.

"But you trusted this French captain?"

"Well, I did at the time. I had no choice, at any rate. He was taking me whether I was willing or not."

"Yet he locked you in a cabin."

"Yes."

"That does not sound like the action of an honorable man."

"No, I guess not. It was all so confusing. I thought we would sail away and I would never see Daniel or you all again."

"It is so fortunate that Frederick saw you taken and followed you."

I nodded.

"About the robe though. How did you come into possession of such a thing? Is this French cloth?"

I had almost begun to relax but stiffened at Mrs. Darymple's words.

Just then we heard a scream. Mrs. Simpson!

CHAPTER FOURTEEN

Mrs. Darymple and I scrambled off the rock ledge and slipped into the water, emerging out from under the waterfall.

Mrs. Simpson huddled in the water, facing us and shrieking. I looked beyond her to where Daniel, Samuel, James and Thomas stood uncertainly, having apparently just returned to camp and unaware that we still bathed.

Daniel rounded up the men and shepherded them toward the huts. He returned, looked at me and pointed to the still-screaming Mrs. Simpson and put a finger to his lips before disappearing again. I understood that he wanted us to calm Mrs. Simpson down.

Mrs. Darymple and I swam toward Mrs. Simpson. Cowering in the water with thin arms covering her chest, she continued to shriek.

"Mrs. Simpson," I said, patting her shoulder. "Please don't scream. The sound carries, and you could give us away."

"Agatha, stop this noise at once!" Mrs. Darymple ordered.

Mrs. Simpson quieted.

"I had no warning," she chattered, seemingly now cold. "They did not announce their presence. For all I knew, they could have been islanders come to kidnap us."

"Well, they weren't. And the men appear to be as embarrassed as we are," Mrs. Darymple said.

The three of us huddled neck deep in the water, looking toward the huts.

"Daniel is a doctor," I said finally. "I doubt he hasn't seen a naked female before."

"Really, Mrs. Wollam, you say the most extraordinary things!" Mrs.

Simpson retorted. She threw a narrow-eyed look over her shoulder toward the huts.

"She is probably right, Agatha. Shall we brave prying eyes and gather our clothing?"

"No, I cannot. I simply cannot."

"Well then, dear, you will simply have to stay in the pool, though you look chilled. I think I will have a nap, and I will check on you when I awaken."

"No! I cannot stay in here alone. If you insist, I will step out. Mrs. Wollam, since you are the most familiar with Dr. Hawthorne, who appears to be our de facto leader, do you think you could ask him to ensure that the men do not attempt to peek?"

"Agatha! How ridiculous!" Mrs. Darymple snapped.

"No, that's fine," I said. "I'll just throw my robe on and return to the huts. I'll keep an eye on them myself, Mrs. Simpson."

"Thank you," she said, lifting her chin in an attempt to look dignified.

I climbed out of the pool and grabbed my robe, absolutely certain that Daniel was keeping an eye on the men. My feet felt better, my hair and skin lightly scented and moisturized if not clean. I limped up to the huts and found the men huddled just outside the last two huts, eating some of the fruit. They had returned with something that looked like breadfruit. As I had expected, the men all had their backs to the pool, though the huts and trees also blocked any view.

Daniel looked up at me, a red stain coloring his cheeks. I smiled, realizing that he was embarrassed.

"Mrs. Simpson sent me up here to ensure that you all don't peek while she and Mrs. Darymple dress. You're back sooner than I expected. Is that breadfruit?"

"Yes," Daniel said. "I gathered some leaves for your feet and the fruit for food. But I think it must be cooked to be palatable." He looked up at the trees overhead. "I am undecided about setting a fire just yet. I do not want to give away our position or that we are alive."

I sat down next to him.

"What did you find? Was anyone at the beach? Any evidence they had been there?"

"No, we saw nothing, although I have no way of knowing if they came and left. I could no longer see the outrigger canoe and wonder if it swept out to sea or whether they collected it."

"Do you mean the Polynesians?"

"Or the French."

"So you don't think we ought to set fires anytime soon? That's going to make cooking kind of hard."

"I continue to believe that someone will search for us, even if at sea. Smoke could be seen from a passing boat. I think we must wait."

"Aye, I agree, Doctor," Frederick said.

I heard Mrs. Simpson talking as the ladies rounded the corner and appeared before us. Mrs. Simpson had tied her hair up as best she could, given that she appeared to have lost most of her hairpins, but Mrs. Darymple chose to leave hers down. Mrs. Darymple had also hiked her skirt up to just above her ankles by tucking a length into her waistband. For all intents and purposes, it looked like the older woman had gone natural. She was clearly taking to life in the tropics.

Daniel threw me an amused look but said nothing.

"That pool is absolutely refreshing! A veritable fountain of youth. I feel invigorated, years younger," she said.

The same could not be said of Mrs. Simpson, who looked unhappy and slightly embarrassed.

"Forgive me for screaming. I am a modest woman, unaccustomed to bathing in the company of others, and when I saw you—"

She dropped her eyes and sat down at the entrance to their hut.

"Think nothing of it, Mrs. Simpson," Daniel said, rising. "Forgive us for not announcing our return in some other fashion. Perhaps we should have called out, but I do worry that others on the island might hear us, and I think we must keep our voices moderated. Again, forgive me."

He handed Mrs. Simpson a coconut husk filled with shredded coconut, bananas, slices of the little "apples" and berries—a veritable fruit salad.

Frederick handed Mrs. Darymple and me two more coconut shells filled with fruit, having apparently busied himself with preparing a meal for all of us. I ate mine with appreciation and licked my fingers for good measure.

"That was wonderful, Frederick. Thank you so much."

"You're welcome, Mrs. Wollam."

"Yes, quite delightful, young man," Mrs. Darymple said. "What did you discover down at the beach, Daniel?"

"No evidence that anyone had pursued us as of yet. We did not see the outrigger canoe either though, so I am not certain whether it was retrieved or swept out to sea. I did hope it would remain locked in the lagoon by the reef so that any anyone searching for it might think we had all drowned."

"You are saying then that you do not know if the Polynesians and French returned and found nothing? Or that they have not yet arrived? The former would be more advantageous." Mrs. Darymple's pragmatic view of the situation impressed me.

"Yes, the former would be most expedient, but no, I have no inkling. Nothing was disturbed at the encampment. The tide came up in the night and washed away any footprints in the sand, including ours."

"Then we must wait and see," Mrs. Darymple said. "And strive to live as modestly and quietly as possible. No fancy balls and orchestras for you now, Mrs. Simpson! You must eschew those activities for the time being," she said with a broad smile.

Mrs. Simpson, appearing to actually relish her food, looked up, smiled faintly and returned to eating.

Mrs. Darymple turned a bright smile upon us all, and I again marveled at the lightening of Mrs. Darymple's temperament, as if the warm tropical waters, bright sun and dazzling foliage had rejuvenated her.

Mrs. Simpson's demeanor had mellowed following her bath in the pool, with the exception of her screaming episode. Now content to sit and to eat quietly, the perpetual lines of discontent in her face smoothed. Did the pool have magical properties, or were we all simply changing in subtle ways, given our experiences?

Daniel smiled more easily than he had on the ship. Oddly, given the danger that we were most certainly in, he too seemed more relaxed. He continued to leave his shirt collar open, revealing tanned skin at the base of his throat. His wavy dark hair gleamed after his recent visit to the pool, and he casually ran a hand through the unruly locks to push them from his face, unsuccessfully. My heart warmed as I watched boyish curls drop down over his forehead again.

As if Daniel felt me watching him, he turned to look at me. I caught my breath at the intimate warmth in his nut-brown eyes. He met my gaze steadily, and I wondered if he could read my thoughts. My heart thumped, and my face flamed as I turned away.

Did Daniel know how much he meant to me? Could he see that I had fallen madly in love with him?

I eyed him from under my lashes. Still looking at me, he smiled quickly before turning away to respond to a question from Mrs. Darymple.

I retreated into myself, half listening to the hum of conversation but mostly watching Daniel and wondering about our future. The light took on an orange tint signaling the arrival of late afternoon. Dusk would come soon.

Mrs. Simpson noted the lateness of the hour first.

"It will soon be nightfall. Will we set a fire? For safety?"

Daniel shook his head. "I do not think that is wise for now, Mrs. Simpson. We cannot give away our position, or even that we still live. When you speak of a fire for safety, what is it that you fear?"

She looked around the jungle with wide eyes.

"Wild animals? The boars you spoke of?"

I wasn't about to mention the wild pig. Not to the worried Mrs. Simpson. Not to the men.

I heard Daniel attempting to reassure Mrs. Simpson as I rose restlessly, pulled my robe more closely around me and limped away from the group. Most of them probably assumed I was going to relieve myself, but I simply wanted to get some air. In my old life—seemingly so far away—I had enjoyed a great deal of solitude. I wondered how I was going to manage in such close quarters. Even the huts had been built within a few feet of each other.

I left the encampment and made my way to the pool, lowering myself to the rocks to dangle my aching feet in the water.

I waited, knowing Daniel would join me soon. He wasted no time and arrived within a few minutes. Sitting down next to me on the ledge, he pulled off his boots and socks to drop his feet into the water.

"I wondered at your expression a few moments ago, Maggie. Is something wrong? Are you worried?"

I turned to look at him. Handsome, nurturing and charming. The look of concern in his eyes pulled at my heart.

"I'm always worried, Daniel. I'm probably more like Mrs. Simpson than I am Mrs. Darymple, who, by the way, appears to be thriving on the island. As do you." I turned away to watch the waterfall, hoping he wouldn't see the blatant infatuation in my eyes.

"I cannot tell you not to fret, dearest. One should worry in our circumstances. But I can tell you, Maggie, that I will protect you with my life."

I caught my breath at Daniel's words. He took my hand in his and brought it to his lips. His kiss, tender and warm, sent a thrill up my arm. My heart raced as he slid the palm of my hand over to his cheek, pressing it there for a moment and gazing at me with a tender expression.

"I love you, Margaret Wollam. I would ask you to marry me, but I do not know how I could find a minister." His tanned face bronzed, and he lowered my hand but did not let go.

"Nor do I know if you would accept my suit. Would you? Would you do me the honor of becoming my wife? Someday?"

His lips curved on the last word, as if to take the sting from it.

I didn't want to dwell on the impossibility of marrying a man on a remote island in the South Pacific—in the absence of a minister or a justice of the peace, in a century not my own, while in hiding from those who might separate us. I didn't want to think about any of the reasons why we couldn't marry.

I laced my fingers through Daniel's and squeezed.

"Yes. Yes, I'll marry you. I love you too, probably from the first time I met you."

Daniel leaned over, slipped his hand behind my neck and pulled me to him. His tender kiss filled me with love—love for him, love for the island, love for life. I wanted it to last forever.

A cough from somewhere nearby broke the spell, and Daniel pulled away, albeit slowly.

"I trust you have honorable intentions, Dr. Hawthorne?" Mrs. Darymple said with a broad grin. She stood behind us, a shocked Mrs. Simpson at her side. The three men and Thomas watched us with varying shades of embarrassment.

Daniel held his own.

"Please congratulate us. I have asked Mrs. Wollam to become my wife—although I am at present uncertain how we can formalize the marriage."

My face burned, but I drew strength from Daniel's confident smile.

"Felicitations!" Mrs. Darymple said, as if we stood in a drawing room.

"Yes, of course, wonderful news," Mrs. Simpson echoed, her expression belying her words.

The men hemmed and hawed their congratulations, while Thomas looked generally uncomfortable with the subject. Thankfully, no one pursued the theoretical impossibility of finding someone to marry Daniel and me, for which I was grateful.

"Come. We do not wish to intrude upon their happy moment," Mrs. Darymple said, shepherding the group back toward the huts. "Do not delay, you two. Dusk is upon us, and darkness will envelop the area."

"Yes, of course, Mrs. Darymple. Thank you. We will return to the camp momentarily," Daniel said with a chuckle.

Suddenly shy, I kept my eyes on our companions as they moved away into the fading light. Daniel pulled me to him again.

"I love you," he repeated. My heart felt as if it would burst at the magical sound of his words.

"I love you too, Daniel."

A crashing sound in the brush opposite the camp caught our ears, and we stiffened. My little pig ran out into the open and stopped short when he saw us.

"A boar!" Daniel exclaimed. He jumped to his feet, as if to chase the poor thing.

"No!" I shouted, rising. The boar saw Daniel and ran back into the jungle the same way it had come.

"No! Leave him alone. Don't chase him!" I grabbed Daniel's arm. He looked down at me.

"But it's a boar!" Daniel said. "Food."

"No," I muttered. "He's just a little hairy pig. Or she. Let him go."

Daniel covered my hand with his own and patted it.

"Maggie, my dear. It is not a pet. We need food sources."

"I know. I know," I said. "But not this little guy. Don't tell the others about him."

Daniel turned to me and took my shoulders in his.

"Did you know there was a boar nearby? Had you seen him already?"

"Yes," I said, hanging my head. "I saw him earlier."

"And you said nothing."

"No. I didn't want you all to kill it."

Daniel pulled me into his arms, and I buried myself in his embrace.

"Silly," he said. "We cannot live on fruit alone."

"No, of course not," I mumbled into his chest. His heart beat strong, if a little fast.

"Will you object when we bring back fish?"

I looked up at him. Even in the low light, his teeth gleamed as he smiled down at me.

"No," I mumbled. "Just not this little guy. Promise me you won't let the men kill him if they see him?" I nodded in the direction of the camp.

"Inasmuch as I have it in my power to control such, I promise, my sweet."

I thrilled to the term of endearment as much as I did to his promise.

Darkness surrounded us now, not pitch black but a soft charcoal. The sound of the waterfall intensified. Birds quieted.

I felt Daniel's fingers under my chin, lifting my face to his. He kissed me slowly. A shiver ran down my spine, and once again I contemplated our possible future.

"We have no way to get married," I said as our lips parted. My statement was meant to be practical rather than an obstruction of future plans. A justice of the peace would have been nice, a minister great, but in the absence of either, I thought Daniel and I should move forward. His next words disappointed me.

"No, we do not have the means to marry, not for the foreseeable future. I am so very sorry, Maggie. I should not have asked you to marry me when I knew we had no way to do so, yet I gave in to my baser instinct to bind you to me, to tell you how very much you mean to me."

I opened my mouth to speak. Nothing came out but a sigh.

"Do you forgive me?"

"There's nothing to forgive, Daniel." I bit my lip and spoke frankly. "Do we have to wait for a minister to marry us?" Even in the growing coolness of the evening, I felt my cheeks burn.

Daniel, now holding my hand once again, squeezed it.

"Yes, dearest. I am afraid we must. I love and respect you too much to sully your reputation."

"My reputation," I said dully.

"Yes."

"Here on the island, with no one about."

"Even here. Mrs. Darymple and Mrs. Simpson would comment. The men would comment."

"I don't care what they say!"

"But I care what they say about you, Maggie. We *will* find a way to marry someday, I promise. Until then I will love you with every fiber of my being."

Before I could argue further, Daniel pulled me to him and kissed me thoroughly.

CHAPTER FIFTEEN

I opened my eyes at the sound of movement through the nearby brush. I'd been wide awake, unable to sleep for the past few hours since Daniel left me at my hut with a chaste, though sweet, kiss to my forehead.

The pig? I crawled to the doorway of my hut and looked out, hoping to see the little guy.

I saw nothing in the darkness though, a faint sliver of moonlight doing little to illuminate the jungle. I emerged from my hut to scan the area for the pig. Apparently, we had squatted on his territory. Either that or he smelled an easy meal from the fruit the men had gathered.

Another rustle in the brush to the right caught my ear, and I turned toward the sound. I shuffled forward in that direction, leaving the encampment. What sorts of sounds did little boars make? Did they grunt? If so, the pig was remarkably silent.

I stopped abruptly, wondering what I had been thinking. I should have awakened Daniel, not wandered into the jungle on my own. As I turned to retreat to the safety of the camp, the bushes rustled again and a hand clamped over my mouth.

Kaihau! I fought against the arms that imprisoned me. Lifted off my feet, I twisted and turned. Whispered French curses caught my attention. Shocked, I stopped struggling momentarily.

Two shadowy figures held me, one under my arms and the other holding my feet. A third figure slid a cloth over my mouth and tied it at the back of my head. I renewed my struggles.

"*Madame*, desist!" a French accent growled in my ear.

The French! It was the French. Captain Sebastian had found us.

I tried to shriek, but whatever sounds I made stuck inside my throat.

Though the night was modestly dark, someone pulled something over my head, blotting out even the faint moonlight. The smell of burlap overwhelmed me. A weight hit me in the stomach, and I realized that I had been thrown over someone's shoulder. My head dangled, and blood rushed to my brain. I waved my arms and kicked until I felt both my arms and feet bound and restrained.

I screamed inwardly as my captors moved quickly, and I bounced mercilessly on someone's shoulder. Pain shot through my stomach, my ribs.

It seemed like we traveled forever. When I thought I couldn't bear any more pain, my captors stopped. I was lowered and dropped onto my right hip on soft ground, perhaps sand. Through my head covering, I heard the sound of waves and French voices.

Someone lifted me to a sitting position and pulled the bag from my head. Captain Sebastian, on his knees at my side, untied the distasteful rag from around my mouth.

"*Madame* Wollam, we meet again," he said smoothly. I scanned my surroundings. The French had carried me back to the beach. I could see our original huts to my left. The French ship lay anchored offshore, just outside of the lagoon. Several small skiffs had been dragged up onto the beach.

"What do you want with me? Why can't you let me go?" I begged. Some of his men sat down in a semicircle, while others stood and watched. The moonlight reflected on the hilts of pistols and knives stuffed into their belts. Francois knelt to untie the strips of cloth that bound my hands and feet.

"Ah! *Madame*, I did let you go once. I made no attempt to pursue you, though I suspected you had not gone far."

"Then why are you here? What do you want?" I rubbed my wrists and eyed Francois, who looked a bit ashamed as he sat back. Had he been the one who carried me?

Captain Sebastian shifted from his knees to a sitting position on the sand.

"I must admit to some surprise when we found you at the oasis. Did your group build these little cottages?" He nodded in the direction of the A-line huts.

"Yes."

"But why, if you do not stay in them?"

"Because we were hiding from you...and Kaihau."

"Ah! Kaihau. Yes, he was most unhappy to discover that you had fled. I did try to explain the situation with his lady, but he did not believe me."

"Why are you here? What do you want?"

"How many men are with you?" he asked, ignoring my question.

I hesitated for an instant, quickly counting his men. About eight.

"Twenty," I said brazenly.

The moonlight shone on Captain Sebastian's bright smile.

"Come now, *madame*! In four huts? Notwithstanding that you most likely have your own quarters?"

"Twenty," I repeated stubbornly.

"Perhaps four?"

"I'm telling you—twenty." I wasn't about to mention the women.

"Very well, *madame*. As you wish. I will have to send to my ship for more men."

"Why?" I burst out. "What for?"

"To restrain this large army of twenty while we seek to accomplish our task."

"Task? Why are you here?" I repeated like a broken record.

"We left some things at the pool, which we must now retrieve."

"Things? At the pool? What things? There's nothing there." I desperately hoped they weren't going for the pig.

"Things that belong to us," he said.

"The pig?" I squeaked.

"Pig?" Captain Sebastian repeated with an obviously confused shake of his head.

I nodded.

"Is there a pig running loose there? No, we are not in search of an animal."

"Don't hurt them," I said, referring to the men and women. "Can't you just get what you need?"

"We were attempting to do so when we discovered you wandering about in the darkness."

"So if you go find what you need, you'll leave us? You won't tell Kaihau that we're here?"

"We found the outrigger canoe that you stole. Several of my men rowed it back to the village. I believe you meant for Kaihau to think you dead? At the moment, he does."

"Thank goodness!" I said, breathing a deep sigh of relief.

"You cannot hide on this island forever, *madame*. Kaihau will soon discover that you live."

Francois spoke then, in French.

Captain Sebastian responded. I understood nothing.

"How many of you are there?" Captain Sebastian asked again. "Francois has suggested that I offer you and your group passage to Tahiti, as I offered before. But I cannot take twenty men."

I hesitated. We could leave the island, all of us. Frankly, I was more convinced than ever that Captain Sebastian was a fair man, no matter what Daniel had heard about him.

With the uncertainty about Kaihau's authoritarianism and his arbitrary kidnapping of me, I doubted our future on Leakiki.

"Four men, a boy and three women, including me," I said promptly. "The other ladies are advanced in age. Do not even think about misusing them." I narrowed my eyes and nodded toward the men.

Captain Sebastian reared his head back, as if startled.

"*Madame*! I take offense. We do not savage women." A flash of teeth showed that he was more amused than angry.

"So you'll take us to Tahiti?"

"Yes, safely."

"Why would you do that?" I asked.

"I do not think you belong here, *madame*. These remote islands are not particularly hospitable to strangers."

"We don't have any money. That I'm aware of." I wasn't about to offer up Mrs. Darymple's money.

"No need to pay for passage. It will be my honor to transport you."

"I still don't understand why you would do that," I said, scrunching my face. "I'm suspicious that you have ulterior motives, but I don't know what they are." Perhaps I was foolish for looking a gift horse in the mouth.

Captain Sebastian reached out to move a lock of hair from my face. I flinched.

"Don't. I'm engaged to be married!" I blurted out.

Captain Sebastian dropped his hand and blinked.

"I meant no disrespect, *madame*. Felicitations. You are affianced to the man who took you from my ship, I presume?"

"Yes."

I glanced at Francois, who looked away, as if uncomfortable. I returned my attention to the captain, who rose.

"I am pleased to transport your entire group to Tahiti if that is your wish, but first we have business to attend to, and that business is near your encampment. We will either take your companions prisoner until we complete our task, or you may speak to your fiancé, and he can guarantee us that he will not try to interfere with our undertaking. Which would you prefer?"

Captain Sebastian extended a hand to help me rise, and I took it, cinching my robe tightly around my waist.

"I'll talk to him. I can go back now."

"Yes, we would like to return to the ship before dawn so that we can set sail. We will accompany you, of course."

Francois called the other sailors. Without asking, he swooped me up into his arms and led the way back down the trail toward the encampment.

"I can walk," I mumbled.

"We do not have time for what must be a painful endeavor, *madame*," Captain Sebastian said. "Francois is pleased to assist. Unless you would rather one of the other men?"

"No!"

Francois's lips twitched, but he said nothing. To his credit, he carried me the entire way in his arms without complaint, though I knew he struggled at times.

Captain Sebastian walked behind us. Just before we reached the oasis, Captain Sebastian called out softly to stop. Francois set me down, lending me an arm while I struggled for balance.

"Please warn your companions that we are not here to do battle, *Madame* Wollam, but if we must, we will. My men can just as easily kill them as not. Are they armed?"

I didn't know how to answer. I suspected Daniel, James, Frederick and Samuel would fight to protect us. Probably even young Thomas.

"I'll talk to them," I said urgently. "Please don't hurt them."

"Very well," he said.

"So should I go?"

He nodded. "Yes, we will await you here."

I nodded and moved past the men on the path to enter the encampment. I peeked into the huts until I found Daniel's. Thomas lay next to him on a mat, curled into a fetal position. I knelt at the opening and tugged at Daniel's booted foot.

He came awake instantly, as if only half asleep, saw me and crawled out of the hut. He put his arms on my shoulders.

"What is it, Maggie?"

I started shaking then, adrenaline receding or surging, I didn't know which. My voice shook, and I stammered, looking over my shoulder the entire time I spoke.

"Cap...Captain Sebastian is he...here! He found us."

Daniel jerked as if to take action, and I grabbed his arms. "No, wait! He's not going to hurt us. He wants something that's around here. I don't know what, a task. But he won't hurt us if we don't resist. He'll give us passage to Tahiti. I trust him, kind of."

"Where is he?" Daniel looked over my shoulder.

"They're nearby, within sight. Please don't do anything, Daniel. You'll endanger the women, Thomas. He's not going to hurt us. He just wants something."

"What? What does he want?"

"I don't know. Something around here."

"Do you expect me to allow him to march in here?"

I nodded vehemently "Yes. There are about twenty of them, and they're armed with knives and pistols."

Daniel pulled me into his arms and hugged me fiercely.

"I am reminded once again that I cannot protect you. I cannot protect the others."

"He'll give us passage to Tahiti, Daniel. I don't think we're in any danger."

"You are so naïve, my dear."

"Maybe. I have to go tell them everything is all right. They're waiting."

Daniel nodded, his shoulders slumped. "I'll awaken the others so they are not taken by surprise."

I turned away and headed back into the jungle. Captain Sebastian rested on a fallen tree. His men squatted on the ground. The captain rose as I approached.

"Okay, Dr. Hawthorne is going to awaken the others and let them know."

"A doctor?" Captain Sebastian echoed. "I thought the man who stole aboard my ship must have been a mariner, a ship's officer."

"He is, but he's a doctor."

"A resourceful one."

"Yes."

"Let us meet your group then. Time flies, and dawn will come soon. I want to conclude my business before first light."

"Why?"

"You ask far too many questions, *madame*. We must make haste, for I do not want the Polynesians to see my ship anchored offshore. They believe we left the island. It is not unusual for them to send canoes out to fish early in the mornings. I wish to be gone before then."

"So you're hiding from the Polynesians?"

Captain Sebastian put a hand on the small of my back to urge me forward.

"Often," he said with an ironic smile. "We have long used this island to...em...store things as we transit the seas, things we have collected along the way that we do not wish the French government to discover or appropriate. Souvenirs, you understand."

Before I could reply, we stepped into the camp. The men and Thomas stood outside their huts. Daniel stood in front of the group, as if protecting them. I noted the women were missing.

"Dr. Hawthorne." Captain Sebastian almost purred.

"Captain Sebastian," Daniel responded. "Your reputation precedes you."

"I have heard of this reputation. Highly exaggerated, I assure you." Captain Sebastian moved forward slowly with an extended hand, as if in a Paris drawing room instead of a moonlit jungle.

"May I extend my congratulations on your engagement to *Madame* Wollam?"

Daniel looked surprised but took his hand.

"Thank you. Mrs. Wollam says you have some business in this area?"

"Yes, we do, and I will dispatch my men to their task while we visit." He turned and spoke to Francois in French, who moved away toward the pool with his men. I wanted to follow to see where the sailors headed, and in fact had turned in that direction, when Captain Sebastian called me back.

"No, *madame*," Captain Sebastian said. "For your safety, you must stay with us."

"What sort of business do French sailors have here, Captain Sebastian, in the dark of night?" Daniel asked.

"The sort that requires the protection of darkness, Dr. Hawthorne. Did *Madame* Wollam tell you of my offer to transport your party to Tahiti?"

"She did. I have not discussed it with the other members of our group, but I suspect that would be most welcome. I would need assurances from you that our group would be unharmed and free to leave upon arrival in Tahiti."

"Of course," Captain Sebastian said with a bow. "Assurances, though, mean little."

Daniel stiffened, and I gasped.

Captain Sebastian laughed. "I am jesting, of course. I honor my word. I have no need of extra crew, especially those who do not speak French, so do not fear conscription." He nodded toward Frederick, Samuel, James and Thomas.

"We have no money," Daniel said. "Why would you offer us passage?"

No one suggested that Mrs. Darymple had offered money earlier.

Captain Sebastian looked at me and shook his head with a grave smile.

"It is small wonder that you asked *Madame* Wollam to marry you. The pair of you think alike." In a voice of exaggerated patience, Captain Sebastian repeated his earlier comments to me.

"Well then, we must gratefully accept your offer," Daniel said. "This island has not been kind to Mrs. Wollam, to say the least, and I do not know what the islanders will do if they find we still live on their island."

"Yes, I wonder the same thing," the captain responded. He heard a sound and turned. We all followed suit to see the men returning. Francois led the procession as the eight men, working in pairs, carried four wooden trunks.

"Treasure?" Daniel asked, his voice faint.

CHAPTER SIXTEEN

"I like to think of them as souvenirs." Captain Sebastian laughed. "We must return to the ship. Are you prepared to leave?"

Daniel looked over his shoulder toward the hut where Mrs. Darymple and Mrs. Simpson must have continued to sleep.

"Give us ten minutes, and then we will follow you."

"Very well. Do not delay. We sail before sunrise."

They left, and Daniel turned to me.

"Maggie, could you please arouse the ladies and apprise them of what is happening?"

"Do you feel better after meeting him?" I asked.

"I do not think we have a choice. He seems prepared to leave us here without compunction, but I have wondered how long we can survive if the islanders discover us, if they decide they do not wish to share the island." He looked over at the men, waiting.

"And this is no life for healthy men...or Thomas," Daniel continued. "They must have opportunities to marry and father children."

"And Thomas's family probably thinks he's dead."

"Yes, that is true, though I do not believe he has written to them since they gave him to the captain."

Daniel gave me a gentle nudge. "Go now. Awaken the ladies. Their capacity to sleep through this amazes me."

I moved toward the ladies' hut and peeked in. Mrs. Simpson, lying on her side, snored loudly. But Mrs. Darymple sat up.

"I heard everything," she said. "So it seems we are to leave paradise and sail away with the French." The note of disappointment in her voice was unmistakable.

"Yes, I think they are somewhat trustworthy."

Just then I heard a crashing through the brush, and I swung around to see the pig running across the encampment and jumping into the jungle on the other side. The men jumped out of the way with curses of surprise. Thomas seemed poised to run after it.

"No, Thomas! Let him go!" I shouted. "He belongs here. We can't take him with us anyway."

Thomas turned back without complaint. I asked Mrs. Darymple to awaken Mrs. Simpson and returned to Daniel's side. With nothing to pack and nothing to carry with us, we waited for the women, who weren't long. Mrs. Simpson emerged from the hut, appearing fairly confused while Mrs. Darymple spoke to her in a low voice.

"No, I am certain that I do *not* understand, Mrs. Darymple, but if we must move again, then we must."

I suspected that Mrs. Darymple hadn't had the time to explain the situation fully to her companion.

"Shall we?" Daniel asked the group. He slipped an arm under my waist to help me. With nods of ascent, the group followed Daniel down the trail back toward the beach. I threw one last look over my shoulder toward the pool, wondering where the French had hidden their treasure.

The little boar emerged into our encampment, watching us walk away. I gave it a small wave and turned my head forward.

The sky lightened as we walked, our progress slow because of me, and by the time we reached the beach, a hazy gray sky greeted us, filled with unshed moisture. Francois awaited us by one of the boats, two of the chests aboard. Captain Sebastian had already shoved off from shore with about four of the sailors. He had apparently left us two men.

"We do not wish to overload the boat. Your men must row," Francois said to Daniel.

"Yes, of course," Daniel replied. "I will row as well. Mrs. Darymple, Mrs. Simpson, if you please?" The older women were lifted over the side of the boat and settled on a bench in the middle, behind the two chests. Daniel picked me up and set me down inside the boat next to the ladies. I turned to study the chests, two plain unassuming boxes of unvarnished oak with metal locks securing them closed.

Thomas climbed in behind us, as did Daniel to grab an oar. The rest of the men pushed the boat into the water, and we followed Captain Sebastian toward his ship.

A patter of rain began soaking us, to Mrs. Simpson's dismay. However, the coolness of the night had passed, and the rain refreshed.

We reached the ship in fifteen minutes and spent the next half hour getting the ladies up the rope ladder. It necessitated that each woman climb onto the backs of Frederick and Samuel.

No matter how much my feet hurt, I wasn't about to ride piggyback up the rope ladder, and I managed to successfully reach the railing of the ship, with Daniel right behind me. The front of my robe flapped open as I climbed over the railing, and I grabbed at it with one hand. I lost my grip on the railing and fell onto the deck, bouncing my head on the hard wood. The pale light of dawn grew dark once again as the world swirled before me.

I didn't know how much time passed before I opened my eyes. I lay upon a canvas chair on an outside promenade deck on a modern-day cruise ship. The orange-and-white lifesaver hooked to the railing proclaimed the ship as the *Century Star*. The back of my head smarted, and I raised a hand to massage it.

With a gasp, I scrambled to my feet to search the deck. A wave of nausea hit me. People strolled by, the women dressed in shorts and knee-length yoga pants, the men in light-colored deck shorts and island shirts. I barely noticed the odd looks thrown in my direction.

No, I was definitely back in the twenty-first century. I clutched my robe closed and ran on tender bare feet down the length of the deck and into the elevator. For a moment I couldn't remember where my cabin was. It seemed as if years had passed since I'd been there.

I emerged from the elevator and ran down the carpeted hall in the direction of my cabin. Along the way, I had wondered how I was going to get into the room, but thankfully, a cabin steward pushed a cart nearby, and I coaxed him to unlock the door. I rushed into the room and stopped short, wondering what to do next.

I should have known better than to return to the French ship. I *had* known better, but I hadn't had a choice. If nothing else, my theory that I traveled through time on ships, but not small boats, had certainly been proven. And apparently, I didn't really have to sleep so much as be unconscious in one form or another.

I moved to the balcony and opened the sliding door, regretting that I hadn't asked the cabin steward where we were. A crisp blue sea drifted past the ship, whitecaps shining under the sun. No land was in sight. Returning to the cabin, I noted it was 11:00 a.m.

I sank down onto the bed and contemplated forcing myself to sleep to see if I could get back to Daniel. I knew Daniel would realize what had happened to me, but I couldn't imagine how he would explain my disappearance. Where was he now? On his way to Tahiti? Where was I?

I looked down at my filthy robe. If nothing else, I needed to shower and find food. As I had before, I called room service and stepped into the shower. I shampooed as if it was the last time I would ever experience hot and cold running water, then emerged to rummage in my luggage for something that would last me a lifetime.

I selected my favorite sports bra, then grabbed another and slid it on over the first bra. I would have grabbed a third but could barely breathe in two of them. Three pairs of panties later, I contemplated my selection of cruise-appropriate clothing. T-shirts and shorts, plus one pair of black yoga pants. I pulled a pair of shorts over the yoga pants and had just slipped into my third T-shirt when a knock at the door announced room service.

Following a delicious last meal of a hot sandwich and fries, I stood, feeling like the Pillsbury Doughboy, swaddled in clothing as I was. Waddling over to my luggage, I surveyed my shoes. I slipped into a lightweight pair of athletic shoes and picked up my last pair of flip-flops to shove into the back of my multiple waistbands. After pulling my still-wet hair up into a ponytail, I stuffed a few extra ponytail holders into one of my shorts pockets and returned to the main cabin to close the balcony curtains.

I lay down on the bed in the darkened room and wished myself to sleep. The flip-flops dug into my back, and I rotated onto my side. Willing myself to sleep again, I thought about Daniel, imagining his tanned wide forehead, bright smile and the shining dark hair that curled just below his ears.

Silently, I called out to him.

Daniel! Daniel.

I steadied my breathing and inhaled deeply to take in more oxygen. I relaxed my eyelids and consciously allowed my mouth to go slack. Trying to ignore an itch on my leg and the urge to open my eyes, I silently chanted Daniel's name over and over, like a mantra.

I lay on the bed for what seemed like hours—full of undigested food, suffocating in layers of clothing, and terrified I might not be able to get back to Daniel.

Finally, I opened my eyes to look at the clock: 3:00 p.m. It had been hours since I'd closed my eyes. A dark hopelessness gripped me, and hot tears spilled from the corners of my eyes.

I imagined Daniel looking for me, waiting for me. No, I couldn't give up. I had to keep trying to get back to him. I pressed my eyelids shut again and concentrated on the memory of Daniel's warm brown gaze.

In the quiet room, I could hear my pulse pounding in my ears. I suspected I was too anxious, too overwrought to sleep. I imagined cute little sheep jumping over a fence, and while the scene amused, I couldn't help wonder why the sheep were jumping over a bit of fencing. Perhaps to get to the other side.

"Daniel," I whispered aloud. "Where are you?"

I remembered sitting with him by the edge of the pool, the delightful silky feel of the warm water on my skin.

I fell over the cliff into sleep.

A familiar creaking sound and the harsh odor of pitch hinted at my location even before I opened my eyes. Sitting up, I recognized the cabin by its resemblance to a closet. I was in the cabin on the French ship. Moonlight filtered in the single porthole, and I swung my legs over the edge of the wooden bunk.

"Daniel!" I whispered urgently. I prayed that I hadn't gone back too far in time, that Daniel was indeed aboard the ship and I wasn't being transported away from him.

I climbed out of the bed and made my way to the cabin door. The ship swayed, and I knew we were underway. I pulled on the door, assuming it was locked, but it opened with a creak. I stepped out into the narrow dark hall before turning left to climb the stairs leading to the deck.

A cool breeze hit me as I neared the top. I stepped out and walked straight into the arms of Captain Sebastian.

"*Madame* Wollam! Is it you?" He held me out at arm's length and looked me up and down with narrowed eyes.

"Where have you been, *madame*? Where did you go? You found some clothing, I see. Where have you been?"

"I can't say," I mumbled, pulling from his grasp. He let me go but continued to run his eyes up and down my body.

"What do you mean you cannot say? You vanished right before our eyes. Simply vanished, and now you have reappeared, dressed in new clothing and altered in appearance."

I looked beyond him. The deck was largely quiet. The moon and stars shone down on us. White sails billowed in the wind.

"Altered?" I mumbled.

"More plump, healthier. Though how this can be over the space of a few hours, I cannot imagine."

"I'm wearing layered clothing."

I looked beyond him again.

121

"Where is Dr. Hawthorne?"

"Not here," Captain Sebastian said.

"What?" I almost shrieked. "Where is he?"

"When you vanished, he refused to leave and returned to the island to await your return, he claimed. Your entire group accompanied him."

"Back to the island! No, he knew if I could come back, it would be to a ship. He must have known that. Didn't we talk about that?"

"What is this? Come back? *Madame*, come and have some cognac to calm yourself. You are obviously in great distress! Your words make no sense!"

"No, I can't," I said, clutching Captain Sebastian's sleeve. "I have to get back to the island. I have to!"

"*Madame*, we are too far out to sea to return to the island now. I think it best you travel with us to Tahiti, as we discussed. Perhaps you can send a ship for Dr. Hawthorne and your companions when you reach Tahiti. If you have the funds, of course."

Money! Where was I going to find money?

"No, please, Captain Sebastian. Please. Take me back to the island. How far away are you?"

"We sailed at first light, *Madame* Wollam. It is now six in the evening. With tailwinds, we made one hundred fifty miles today. It would take us twice that to return to the island if those winds continue to prevail. The men wish to reach Tahiti to enjoy the fruits of our voyages. I cannot turn back."

Tears streamed down my face. Tahiti! What was I going to do in Tahiti without money? Without Daniel?

I dragged in a deep breath to steady myself. I supposed all I really needed to extricate myself from this mess was to return to the cabin and go back to sleep. If I did that though, I probably had no chance of getting back to Daniel, none. I needed a ship in the nineteenth century.

"How far is Tahiti?"

"Please do not weep, *Madame* Wollam." The captain extracted a handkerchief from the pocket of his coat. "I cannot bear to see a lady cry. It is approximately six days, perhaps more, perhaps less if we are lucky."

I saw Francois approach and behind him, my old keeper, Jacques. And I remembered Vana, on a nearby island.

"Are there any islands near where we are now? Like the one you said Vana lives on? Where you can drop me off and it won't cost me so much to try and return to Leakiki?"

"We pass close to that island late at night, but it would be a great inconvenience to anchor the ship and take you ashore. What will you do there? Do you have any money to buy a boat? A crew to return you to the island?"

I shook my head.

"No, not a nickel."

"A nickel?"

"No money," I amended.

Captain Sebastian sighed heavily. He looked over his shoulder at Francois and Jacques, then turned back to face me.

"My dear *Madame* Wollam. I fear your tears have touched me. Perhaps I can assist you in this matter," he murmured. "I could give you a small sum to buy a boat, perhaps even to hire a crew, but it seems inconceivable to me that you could actually command such a crew."

Francois cleared his throat and spoke in French. The captain looked at him in surprise. They spoke for a minute, with Jacques adding comments. On exhausted legs, I watched them and tried to pick out words I understood. I heard none other than references to me.

Captain Sebastian turned back to me with a wry expression.

"It seems you have a champion in my first officer. Francois wishes to guide you in purchasing a boat and finding a crew. Jacques has offered to help. I cannot be without both, but Francois insists that a woman alone cannot manage. I am in agreement. I will loan Francois to you for a brief period. He will help you get back to Leakiki."

I turned and looked at the tall man, studiously staring down at his boots.

"Francois! Thank you! Thank you!" I said, throwing myself against him. He stiffened and set me back.

"It is nothing, *madame*. You are very persistent, and I fear for your safety. Though I think the best we can do is an outrigger canoe."

"A canoe? Over open ocean?" I gasped.

"The Polynesians have traveled great distances in the larger outrigger canoes. I will hire some Polynesians to row. Sometimes it is better to row than await fortunate winds."

Captain Sebastian eyed us. "That is settled then. We shall reach Pokulau in a few hours. Perhaps you would care for a meal?"

I shook my head. "I actually just ate. I'll just wait up here if that's all right."

"As you wish, *madame*." Captain Sebastian turned and spoke to Francois and Jacques, who moved off to do whatever he requested. He bowed to me.

"I have some matters to attend to, *Madame* Wollam. Until later."

I nodded and wandered down the deck to find a seat on a wooden storage locker where I could watch the sailors, the stars, the moon and the dark water slip silently by.

As promised, within a few hours, we dropped anchor in a small bay not much larger than the one near the village on Leakiki. I was on my feet and following Francois around long before he was ready to disembark. Before we climbed down the rope ladder to the waiting rowboat, Captain Sebastian pressed a bag of coins in my hand and spoke to Francois.

Returning his attention to me, the captain took my hand in his.

"*Bon chance, Madame* Wollam. It is probably untimely of me to say, but I do regret not meeting you before. One never knows what might have happened between us had we met before your engagement. It is not too late to change your mind?"

CHAPTER SEVENTEEN

"No," I said, my cheeks burning. "I need to get back."

"My loss," he said, released me and pressed a courtly hand over his heart with a smile. "Francois will assist you in whatever you need."

"How does Francois get back to you, to the ship?"

"Francois and I have discussed that. We will return to Leakiki in several months. We will collect him then."

"A couple months?" I repeated.

Francois nodded and spoke. "Do not worry, *madame*. I will occupy myself until they return for me."

I remembered the beautiful women on the island, and I imagined that Francois would do just fine, *if* they allowed the young women out to see Francois.

"Thank you for the money, Captain Sebastian," I said, stuffing the coins into my shorts pocket with difficulty. "I don't know if I can ever repay you, but I can never thank you enough."

"It is my pleasure to assist you, *Madame* Wollam," he said. He took my hand and kissed it before helping me over the railing and onto the rope ladder. My athletic shoes helped considerably.

Francois, carrying a lantern, followed me down into the skiff to join four other sailors, who manned the oars. I could see little of the island in the dark, but the French seemed to know what they were doing. We rowed up onto shore, and two of the men lifted me out of the boat and carried me onto dry sand. I understood enough French to know that the men bid Francois farewell before they pushed the boat back into the water and jumped in to row back to the ship.

"Come, *madame*. We will go into the village." Francois put a hand under my arm and held the lantern as he guided me along a sandy path that led up a hill. He seemed to know his way around, but I couldn't make out much of the landscape in the dark.

We crested the hill, little more than a sand dune really, and came upon a small village of huts, visible only because a few sleepy fires continued to burn.

"The village sleeps," he said. "We will go to the chief." He led me into the village and past several thatched huts, coming to a stop in front of one. He called out in French, and an older man with long silvery hair came to the door and looked out at us.

The man, clearly taken by surprise, came out and greeted Francois. A simple grayish sarong around his waist competed his ensemble. He eyed me with curiosity and spoke to Francoise again.

"*Non,*" said Francois. He turned to me and spoke in English. "*Madame* Wollam, may I present Ikale, chief of this village?"

I nodded and Francois continued.

"He asked if you were my wife, and I said no."

Francois then returned his attention to the chief, who took Francois's lantern from him, as if receiving a gift. I suspected Francois would not get it back, but he seemed unsurprised.

By this time, a tall similarly silver-haired woman came out of the hut. Her sarong covered her upper torso, ending at her knees.

Francois spoke in French, and the couple began talking rapidly, gesturing to me.

"Is this about the boat?" I asked.

"Yes," he said. "And Vana."

"Vana!" I exclaimed.

"Yes, they say they want us to take her back to Leakiki. She is not happy here. Her sailor left her."

"With us?" I asked, visions of a little outrigger canoe getting smaller all the time as we sailed across open ocean.

Francois spoke to the couple, who nodded and responded.

"Yes, they wish to send her back with us. They say her unhappiness is spreading throughout the village, and if we do not take her, they are prepared to send her out to sea on her own. I do not think she could survive."

"Well, of course we'll take her."

Francois nodded and responded to the elderly couple. They beamed, both of them missing a few teeth here and there. They spoke again, gesturing for us to enter the hut. I followed Francois into a hut that shared the same characteristics as those in the village on Leakiki. Woven palm fronds were used as matting and walls. Timbers supported the structure, and palm fronds were used for decoration, often interwoven with flowers.

Surrounded by a ring of rocks, a small fire burned in the middle of the hut. A beautiful young Polynesian woman sat demurely in a corner of the room, her legs tucked beneath her. Her waist-length wavy black hair glowed almost red in the reflection of the fire, or perhaps it was the ruby-red sarong that gave her hair a russet tone.

Lustrous black eyes and full lips formed a sullen expression as she eyed us. She looked me up and down, her eyes widening before she spoke to the older couple in Polynesian.

I looked to Francois, who stared mesmerized at the beauty. Vana, I presumed. Francois looked smitten, and I knew that didn't bode well for the French lieutenant, since Kaihau thought Vana was his girl.

The exchange between the older couple and the young woman sounded sharp, argumentative. The older couple must have prevailed though, because they turned from Vana and pointed to Francois and me to sit. They took seats on mats themselves and directed Vana to serve us with a wooden cup of some sort of delicious fruit juice. Ikale set the lantern down in front of his wife, and together they admired it.

I assumed Vana had been staying with the chief and his wife since her sailor left her and that she had been acting as a servant of some sort. Francois, after an exchange with the older couple, confirmed my thoughts.

"Vana has been waiting upon the chief and his wife in exchange for food and a bed." I looked over at the mat upon which Vana sat, thinking the term "bed" was stretching things a bit.

"She looks angry," I said out of the corner of my mouth while attempting to maintain a pleasant smile.

"She is," he said. "She does not wish to return to Leakiki. She says there is nothing for her there. Kaihau will probably not take her back, and she has no family."

"But she can't stay here?"

"No, several breadfruit trees have died since she arrived, and the village believes she brings ill spirits to them. They want her to leave."

"Poor thing," I said, though it was hard to sympathize with the glowering young woman. I glanced back at Francois, who had returned to staring at her.

"Francois," I whispered. "When can we leave? Did you ask them about a boat or a canoe and a crew?"

Francois dragged his eyes from Vana, glanced at me and nodded. He turned to the older couple and spoke to them in French. They discussed something for a while before Francois spoke to me.

"Give me two of the coins," he said. "They will give us a canoe and four men to row it."

"Two?" I asked. "But I have a whole bag of gold."

"Keep the gold. You may need it someday. Just two coins."

Without pulling the bag from my pocket, I reached in, fingered two coins and extracted them to hand to Francois. The chief and his wife grinned upon receiving the coins.

"Can we go now?" I asked.

Francois turned to me, his dark eyebrows raised. "No, *Madame* Wollam. We cannot leave until first light. It is much too dark to set out on such a journey tonight."

"Noooo," I groaned in exasperation. But I knew he was right. If I had been wondering where we were to sleep, the chief's wife answered my question. She pointed to a corner of the hut and spoke to Francois, who translated.

"The chief's wife has graciously invited us to stay in their hut tonight." The bronzing on his tanned angular cheeks could have been from the fire or could have been from heightened emotion as he returned to staring at Vana, who generally ignored him.

"Here? With all these people?" I looked around the hut.

Francois dragged his attention back to me.

"Yes, of course. The Polynesians are happy to share their homes. They are very friendly."

Except for Vana, I thought.

Knowing I wouldn't sleep a wink that night, I acquiesced.

"I need to—" I waggled my eyebrows at Francois, who narrowed his eyes in seeming confusion and shook his head.

"Outside?" I nodded toward the door.

"Ah!" he said, his cheeks continuing to redden. "I am certain that if you go outside to the back of the hut, you will find what you need."

I nodded, my own cheeks red, and I rose to walk to the door. I could hear the people behind me speaking rapidly and assumed they asked where I was going.

I stepped outside and dragged in a breath of fresh air. The village was largely quiet, but I could see the embers of a few fires and hear a smattering of voices. I walked around to the back of the hut and by odor detected the appropriate area. I would have killed for a real outhouse but made do with a pit carved into lava rock.

I jumped up and retreated from the area, reluctant to return to the hut. Still, with no idea of where to wander in the darkness, I made my way back to the front of the hut, where I found Francois awaiting me, having apparently managed to tear himself away from Vana.

"Did you find what you needed?" he asked.

"Yes, thank you." Since I had his attention, I asked a question.

"Are we all just going to sleep together in there? Not in a huddle, right?"

Francois laughed. "Yes, *madame*, we will sleep inside the hut, but not in a huddle, I promise. I hope you do not mind."

"I should be grateful, but I really wish it was morning."

Francois nodded. "If you will excuse me, I will see you inside."

He rounded the hut, and I assumed he was off to relieve himself. I would have preferred to wait for him, but the chief's wife stuck her head out of the hut and with a big wide grin, crooked her fingers and signaled for me to enter. I stepped inside and took up my spot, and the elderly Polynesians and I grinned and nodded at each other until Francois returned. Vana had lain down and turned her back to the room.

"Good night, *madame*. Sleep well," Francois said as he followed Vana's example. The chief extinguished the small fire in the room, said something, and they lay down as well on the opposite side of the room. I lowered myself to a supine position and stared into the darkness with no intention of sleeping in case I accidentally traveled through time.

The muted roar of waves hitting the nearby beach penetrated the silence of the hut, and the rhythmic noise lulled me into a state of drowsiness. I widened my eyes, determined to stay awake. On ship or on dry land, I could not lose my chance to find Daniel, to reunite with him.

I awakened with a start to the feel of a hand shaking my shoulder gently. Pushing myself upright, I looked up to see Francois bending over me.

"It is time to leave, *madame*," he said. Behind him, the rosy glow of dawn spread into the hut through the open doorway.

I nodded, rubbed my thick eyes and pushed myself off the ground. Francois waited and beckoned me outside. The chief, his wife and Vana sat on hewn logs outside, eating food tucked into broad leaves. The elderly woman signaled that I should sit and join them, but Francois shook his head.

"Take the food with you, *madame*," he said. "We must go. The tide is favorable." He spoke to the elderly couple and Vana, no doubt telling them the same thing. Vana wiped her hands on her sarong and stood, with no luggage, no belongings.

She turned and spoke to the older couple in Polynesian, in what sounded like a few curt words that I interpreted to mean "thanks for nothing." Turning a cold shoulder to them, she stalked off toward the beach.

The smiles on their faces revealed no signs of grief, and the chief's wife pressed some wrapped food into my hand. I looked down at the broad leaf in my hand to see what I suspected was mashed breadfruit, banana pieces and some delicious-looking nuts. I couldn't wait to eat it.

She handed Francois a matching packet of food, and he nodded and appeared to thank them.

"Shall we?" he said, turning to me. I nodded and followed him through the village and back down to the beach, eating my food along the way. The portion size was not large, and I finished before we arrived.

Captain Sebastian's ship was long gone. A large outrigger canoe awaited us, much bigger and more elaborate than the one Daniel had scuttled. Resembling a catamaran with double hulls upon which a small domed thatched shelter balanced, a mast jutted up from a length of timber lying across the center, its sail furled. Six short but stocky male islanders stood by, holding oars. Vana had already climbed onto the canoe and crawled into the shelter, ignoring the men who threw curious glances at her.

Since the canoe had been pulled up onto the sand, I was able, with Francois's help, to climb aboard. I took a seat on a narrow bench just in front of the hut and awaited our departure with joy and trepidation.

Francois helped the islanders push the canoe into the water, and then all seven men jumped in at various intervals. The men took up their oars and thrust them into the water, pulling in earnest. I looked forward. We seemed again to be in a lagoon and would have to fight a few waves to get out to open ocean.

Expertly maneuvered by the sturdy Polynesians, the canoe reached the coral reef in no time at all, and rather than flounder in the breaking waves, we sailed over the reef and into the sea with ease. I had barely managed to grab my bench seat before the whitewater surfing was over.

Francois turned and looked over his shoulder, I presumed to see if I was still there, and I nodded. I saw his gaze move beyond me, and I turned to see Vana lying down, apparently napping. I found her entitled behavior unpleasant, but upon meeting Francois's bedazzled eyes once again, I saw that I was alone in that opinion.

The sea was fairly calm with no whitecaps visible. I watched Pokulau recede in the distance, a small island featuring gently rounded hills in contrast to the jagged peaks of Leakiki.

My eyelids started to droop as the canoe moved through the gentle swells, and I almost fell off my bench once, catching myself just in time.

I rose, eyed Vana with envy, and decided to join her under the shelter. She didn't waken as I slid in next to her. My last thought before I fell asleep was mild surprise that I didn't travel through time.

I awakened some time later at the sound of tapping, as if someone tapped on the door.

CHAPTER EIGHTEEN

I opened my eyes. Just outside the shelter, one of the men tapped on a coconut with a machete. A gentle rocking beneath me confirmed that I was still on the outrigger canoe. I sat up, noting that Vana still slept beside me.

The islander, brawny and handsome with lustrous black hair pulled back from his face, looked up and saw me. Tattoos decorated all visible skin. He smiled and handed me the coconut from which he had pared an opening. He made a universal gesture of drinking, and I took the coconut from him and drank the sweet nutritious liquid.

Francois appeared at his side, took another coconut from a pile at the Polynesian's knees and handed it to him. Fully expecting Francois to drink from the coconut, I was surprised to see him move toward the shelter, kneel down and gently touch Vana on the foot.

When Vana didn't waken, Francois shook her foot yet again. Vana finally sat up, rubbing her eyes. She took the proffered coconut from Francois without a word and drank from it.

Francois turned away, rose and accepted another coconut, which he drank from this time.

"Where are we?" I asked. "How much farther?"

Francois looked up at the billowing sails. It was then that I noted almost all the islanders lounged or slept except for one at a tiller.

"If the wind holds steady at our backs, perhaps a few more hours," he said. "We caught a favorable current and will make better time returning to Leakiki."

"A few more hours? Really?" My heart pounded. Just a few more hours? "How long did I sleep?"

"Many hours," Francois said. "Vana even longer." He nodded toward Vana, who looked up as he spoke her name. Her lips evened out into a semblance of a smile, albeit not a very warm one. Francois's cheeks bronzed.

We drank, ate the food that the islanders had kindly brought and generally relaxed while the wind did the work. If I had worried that the canoe couldn't handle open sea, I was mistaken, especially given the current that Francois had described.

The next few hours passed slowly, and the sun began to descend. The wind shifted, and the men furled the sail and returned to rowing. Vana lounged on deck, watching the activities with little interest. I didn't even try to talk to her. What Francois saw in her, I couldn't understand. Certainly not her personality.

I moved over to sit beside Francois.

"It's going to be dark soon," I fretted. "How will you see the island?"

Francois nodded, his lips pressed together.

"I had hoped Leakiki would be in sight now, but I do not see it."

"What if we miss it?"

"Please do not worry, *madame*. It will not help and will only upset you. I believe we are on the appropriate heading." He rested his oar on his lap and pulled out a compass to consult it.

"Yes, we are on course. Perhaps I overestimated our speed. I could not say for certain in the canoe."

I bit my lip and scanned the horizon in search of land, some sort of dark shape, but could see nothing. It was as if I experienced déjà vu, only Daniel was not by my side.

Francois resumed rowing. I sat by him for the next hour as the sun dropped out of sight. The sunset, a splendid display of orange, purple, red and yellow streaks, failed to move me since I knew that darkness would soon follow.

There were no lamps on the canoe, and night fell in earnest. In the absence of visual stimulus, I heard only the sound of the oars slapping rhythmically against the water, the canoe cleaving through the sea. Either the moon had not yet risen or it would not shine that night.

Vana startled me by appearing at my side. She took a seat on the bench next to me and stared into the night.

No wind broke the silence. The men did not speak. I didn't beg Francois for more pointless reassurances. The absence of sound was eerie, the absence of light terrifying.

A piercing shriek startled me, and I responded in kind. But my scream was shrill, unlike the hoarse cries of some kind of bird. Other birds chimed in, as if we had awakened them.

"We are near land," Francois said. "But I cannot be certain it is Leakiki."

I had been just about to sing out thankful praise when Francois's words sent me into a tailspin. I watched as one of the islanders rose and scanned the darkness. I stood as well to see over their heads, but could see nothing, nothing but blackness.

The lookout shouted something and pointed. Though I could barely even see him, I managed to follow his arm. In the distance to our right, a small haze of reddish-orange glowed, just a break in the darkness.

Francois called something out in French, and the canoe turned toward the glow.

"What is it?" I asked.

"A flame perhaps from fire, perhaps from lava. I have seen such a light at night in Hawaii, from lava spilling into the sea."

"Lava! Like an eruption?" I gasped. I strained to see the outline of the mountain, to see if flames spewed from one of the peaks, but I saw nothing other than the glow near the horizon.

"No, I think not. Leakiki is a volcanic island, but I do not see any flames from a volcano."

He looked past me to speak to Vana in French, the first time I think he had ever really spoken to her.

"*Non*," she responded. She said a few more things I didn't understand.

"Vana says there is no mountain of fire, only pools where the hot rock burns."

"So is that lava or not over there?" I asked.

Francois shook his head. "I do not know. If it is indeed fire, it is very large, much larger than what we might see from a village campfire."

"A large fire?" My mouth went dry. "What if Kaihau found them? What if he attacked, if he's burning them out?"

Francois spoke to Vana, who shrugged her shoulders rather callously, in my opinion, before responding. She seemed to say a lot. I struggled to breathe as I watched her speak.

"Vana says Kaihau is a great chief, but he has a temper. She does not know what he might do to the older women, but he will probably kill the men."

"What?" I shrieked. "What?"

Francois put a restraining hand on me as I jumped up, prepared to take an oar myself and hurry us to shore.

"Please sit down, *madame*. To be honest, I am not certain that Vana does not exaggerate. She does not seem to like Kaihau much. I have met him on many occasions. He does have a temper—she is right—but he has not yet killed Captain Sebastian or myself."

I took little comfort in his words.

"Please hurry," I whispered. "Please hurry!"

I knew that the islanders had already sped up their rowing, but it didn't seem fast enough. The glow grew in size, but the source was still indistinguishable.

I clung to the bench seat, panting with fear as the canoe swept through the water. The sound of the splashing oars and angry birds soon gave way to the crash of waves. The front of the canoe rose and fell as a current gathered up the canoe and rushed us toward shore. A rim of white formed in the darkness, and I thought I recognized a coral reef.

Francois shouted to the islanders.

"Is it a reef?" I asked.

"Yes," he said curtly, focusing his attention.

It seemed only days ago that our small boat had run aground on the coral reef. I bit my lip and hung on to the bench seat, hoping for the best, and prepared to swim if I had to—if I wasn't dashed against the coral again, if I could swim for the surface in the darkness.

But the islanders were experts at what they did. The canoe raced toward the breaking waves, lifted up and sailed over the reef and into a lagoon of calm water. I looked over my shoulder toward the roaring white line of surf before turning forward to study the yellow-orange glow before us.

"It's fire!" I called out.

"Yes, fire," Francois agreed. He spoke to the islanders in French again, and rather than race toward it, the islanders slowed the canoe and came to a stop in the lagoon, floating quietly.

"What are you doing?" I whispered, intuitively aware that Francois wanted quiet.

"I am not prepared to race into flames, *madame*. We do not know the source of the fire. We will drift in the lagoon until I ascertain the fire's origins."

I looked toward the island. The fire appeared to burn on the beach, a deserted beach. I could not see the village beyond. I saw no outrigger canoes, no huts, no people. What was the purpose of the fire? Other than the flames, the scene appeared remarkably peaceful. It was as if someone lit a bonfire.

"I think it's just a bonfire on the beach," I whispered. "I don't see anyone running around, no screaming or shouting."

"Yes, I see that now," Francois said. He whispered in French and the islanders lifted their oars and maneuvered the canoe toward the beach. Except for the faint splashing of water and the hum of waves as they ebbed and flowed on shore, I heard nothing. Even the birds seemed to have gone back to sleep at sea.

We rowed toward the beach silently, my heart pounding so loud I thought surely everyone could hear. As we neared, I could hear the crackling of the bonfire, which burned bright. Freshly fueled with timber, it had not been left to die. Someone had to be nearby.

Francois silently directed the islanders to climb out and pull the canoe up on shore.

"Stay," he whispered to me. He repeated his command to Vana in French.

I clung to the side of the boat, staring at the fire, studying the beach. Was this the same beach where we had landed only a few days before? Where we had built the huts? The firelight did not extend to the tree line, and I couldn't see the huts.

Francois pulled a knife from a sheath at his hip, the large blade gleaming dangerously in the firelight. The islander who had cut the coconuts brandished his machete. Several others also carried knives. Francois paused, signaling with a raised hand for the islanders to pause. Most of them sank into silent crouches.

The hairs on my head stood up at the deadly sight, and I didn't know what to do. I wanted to shout "Stop!" What I didn't want was warfare. I didn't want to see violence.

I jumped out of the boat and ran up to Francois, who seemed poised, waiting and listening. Upon hearing my footsteps, he whirled around with his knife raised. I ducked and cowered.

"It's me, Francois!" I whispered.

Francois grabbed my arm and pulled me upright.

"*Madame*, why did you not stay in the canoe as I requested? Where is Vana?"

"In the boat," I said. "Please don't start a fight." It was then that I saw the huts outlined in the firelight. "Oh, thank goodness, this is Leakiki! Who set this bonfire?"

"I do not know," he whispered. "We have seen no one yet."

Just then a rustling sound crashed through the underbrush. My little pig ran out of the darkness, stopped short at the sight of us, then ran back into the brush. Daniel appeared out of the darkness, stepping out onto the beach as if he had been walking behind the little guy. He watched the boar disappear, then looked up and saw us.

"Daniel!" I shrieked. "Daniel!" I ran around the fire and across the sand, tripping as I reached him. He scooped me up into his arms and held me against him.

"Maggie, Maggie," he murmured against my ear. "My love, you have come back to me!"

"I've traveled so far, so very far," I said breathlessly. "You have no idea. I traveled back...on the ship...no more ships for me. I love you. I love you."

"And I love you. I am so thankful to see you. You see the fire. I set it every night for you since you disappeared, I set the fire so you could find your way back to me. Oh, my dearest! I love you, Maggie Wollam. You must *not* leave me again. I will *not* let you leave me again." Somehow his words ended in a lecture.

"No! No, never. I won't set foot on another boat again, not even a canoe. Even if I have to spend the rest of my life here on the island, I won't get on another ship."

Daniel lifted his head and ran a tender hand down the side of my face, cupping my chin in his. He bent and kissed me deeply, purposefully, wondrously, and I melted in his arms.

It was at least a full minute before I became aware of Francois coming to our side. I looked up to see him greet Daniel. The islanders relaxed—some dropping to the sand, others exploring the area, the huts in the tree line. Vana climbed out of the boat and emerged into the light of the fire.

Daniel's eyebrows lifted.

"Vana, I presume," he said.

"Yes, she was sent back to the island," Francois said.

"Kaihau will be pleased," Daniel murmured.

"Oh, I don't think so, Daniel," I whispered. "She's just not into him, if you know what I mean."

Daniel tilted his head at my expression, but I thought he understood as I reached up to kiss his cheek. He kept one arm around me as we turned to watch Francois speak to Vana.

"What happened, my love? Where did you go this time?" Daniel bent his head and whispered in my ear.

"Back to the *Century Star* again. I don't know where the ship was exactly, out to sea somewhere. I showered, ate and put on as many clothes as I could."

As I spoke, I reached toward my back, amazed to find the tips of my flip-flops still sticking out of the waistband.

"I did wonder at your newfound fluffiness," he whispered with a chuckle. I rewarded his rudeness with another passionate kiss on his cheek.

"How is everyone? Where are they?"

"At the encampment by the pool. They are well but worried, Mrs. Darymple most of all. She is very fond of you."

"I'm fond of everyone too, especially you, Doctor."

He looked down at my athletic shoes.

"How are your feet?"

"Getting better."

"What sort of shoes are those?"

"Athletic shoes, very lightweight. I hope they last, because like I said, I'm not leaving the island."

I looked over at Francois speaking to Vana and the Polynesians. His gestures to the left indicated he was probably talking about Vana's village.

"Is it your intention then to stay here on the island forever, Maggie?" As if fraught with some profound emotion, Daniel's hushed voice broke.

I turned and looked at him. He had pulled away from me and watched me intently, his dark gaze burning in the firelight. I wanted to wrap my arms around his waist, to nestle back into his embrace, but his rigid stance suddenly frightened me.

"You're scaring me, Daniel," I whispered. "I don't know what the right answer is. What do you want me to say?" I swallowed hard as he stared at me silently.

"Yes, I was going to stay here," I said hurriedly. "I don't know any other way to be with you. Are you planning to leave? Are you saying you won't stay with me?"

Pain ripped at my heart, and I locked my hands behind my back, willing back burning tears. Something had gone terribly wrong in the past few moments. We weren't as one. We did not want the same thing, *need* the same thing.

I could not leave the island, I knew that now. But if Daniel left me, what would be the point of staying? I stared at his beloved face, pleading with my eyes but struggling to remain silent as I waited for his answer. I wanted to beg him to stay, but I couldn't.

Daniel breathed in and then exhaled.

"Yes, of course I will stay with you, my love. Forever, if you will have me. I hoped and prayed that you would want to stay here...on the island. Times will be hard. Life will not be easy, but I cannot risk losing you again. Someday you may not be able to return to me. And that I could not bear. I love you, Maggie. I cannot live without you."

I let go of the breath I'd been holding and flung myself into Daniel's arms.

"Forever," I whispered. "Forever."

"Forever," he echoed against my ear.

CHAPTER NINETEEN

One year later

I looked up from the baby's sleeping face to see my husband approaching from the beach. Tanned, lean, wearing nothing but trousers cut just above the knee, he was the epitome of a handsome heroic castaway on a tropical island—which in a sense he was. Daniel, though, was a castaway of his own volition, as perhaps was I.

Our daughter mewled in her sleep, and I patted her bottom gently as I watched Daniel. He had been scavenging seaweed in the lagoon for me, a delicacy that we dried and used in soups, our own little version of sushi and snacks.

Dropping down onto the sand beside me under the shade of a palm tree, he set down one of my old T-shirts holding the seaweed and took the baby from me.

"How was your haul?" I asked.

"Good," he said. "You shall have your 'dried seaweed snacks' in abundance. You as well, Mrs. Darymple."

I turned to look at Mrs. Darymple, also tanned and looking much younger than her seventy years. She wore her hair caught in a gray ribbon, having long ago chosen to forgo many of the Victorian trappings of her former life.

I remembered the day she had returned from a relaxing swim in the pool only to rip her dress apart at the seams and hand it to me to help her fashion something more suitable to the climate. Hesitantly, I had draped the material about her and over her shoulder like a sarong, and she had delighted in the comfort and ease of the style.

"Yes indeed, I look forward to some dried seaweed," Mrs. Darymple said with a relaxed smile.

I turned to look at Daniel, cradling the baby in his arms and rocking her gently.

"I'd like some salt to go with it though. When did Captain Sebastian say he was returning?"

"In a few weeks," Daniel said.

"Good. It will be nice to see him. I think Francois misses him, but he would miss Vana more if he were to return to sea."

"Yes, I agree with you there," Daniel said.

It had been almost eleven months since Captain Sebastian had returned to the island to pick up Francois. By then Francois had fallen madly in love with Vana, and he had asked permission to leave Captain Sebastian's service and stay on Leakiki.

Kaihau, as it turned out, no longer wanted Vana when he discovered that she had willingly left the island to live with a French sailor, a fact that did not displease Vana. According to Francois, she had never loved Kaihau and had no ambition to become the chief's wife.

Instead, she had become Francois's wife and was about halfway through the pregnancy of their first child.

Daniel and I had struggled to find a solution to his old-fashioned notion that we must marry. I had been more flexible about the arrangement, but he had refused more than just exchanges of passionate, albeit chaste, kisses until we married.

When Captain Sebastian returned to collect Francois, Daniel had asked him if he knew of any missionaries or priests in the area. To our delight, Captain Sebastian said that he would marry us himself. I refused to board his ship to do so, and although he didn't understand why, he consented to marry us out in the lagoon on one of the outrigger canoes, flower laden, in the most romantic sunset wedding I could have imagined.

Captain Sebastian, warmed up, had gone on to marry Francois and Vana the following day, and even Frederick, who had fallen madly in love with a village girl at first sight.

James and Samuel, who also lived in the village with Frederick and his wife, were "dating" two village girls, sisters. Thomas continued to live with us at the encampment near the pool, having cleaved to Mrs. Darymple on the departure of Mrs. Simpson.

"Perhaps Captain Sebastian will bring news of Mrs. Simpson, a letter," Mrs. Darymple said, breaking the comfortable silence that had fallen on us.

"I hope so. I know how worried you are," I said.

"She was very unhappy here," Mrs. Darymple said with a sigh, "but she tried very hard."

"Indeed," Daniel said.

I thought back to Mrs. Simpson, who had sailed away with Captain Sebastian after the weddings. She truly hadn't taken well to the South Pacific, and she wanted to return to San Francisco. Mrs. Darymple, on the other hand, thrived and couldn't bear to leave. So they had parted ways. I thought Mrs. Darymple much happier without her but never said so.

"Where is that boy?" Mrs. Darymple asked, reaching up to shade her eyes as she looked out to sea. At that moment a small outrigger canoe entered the lagoon from the west. Even from here I could see the sun-bleached strands of Thomas's hair as he paddled the canoe. Joining him was a friend he had made some months before, a Polynesian youth of around the same age.

Thomas had left that morning to row through the lagoon around to the other side of the island to pick up a few things. Mrs. Darymple was very fond of Aikane's breadfruit chips, and Aikane was always happy to oblige.

Contrary to Vana's threats, Kaihau was disinclined to care about our presence on the island. He had moved on and was now happily married to another woman. Apparently marriage had improved his disposition.

A sound in the underbrush caught my ear, and I turned to see Piggy emerge. He sauntered up to us, having lost all his earlier wariness, and he stopped at Daniel's side to sniff the baby's hair. I handed Daniel half a banana to give Piggy, and then we all turned to watch Thomas and his friend row toward shore.

Daniel had told me life would be hard, and it had been, but not as hard as sailing away on a ship and out of his life. I reached over to kiss Daniel's bearded cheek with deep and profound contentment.

"Forever," he whispered with a glance at me.

"Forever," I said

ABOUT THE AUTHOR

Bess McBride is the best-selling author of over fifteen time travel romances as well as contemporary, historical, romantic suspense and light paranormal romances. She loves to hear from readers, and you can contact her at bessmcbride@gmail.com or visit her website at www.bessmcbride.com, as well as connect with her on Facebook and Twitter. She also writes short cozy mysteries as Minnie Crockwell, and you can find her website at minniecrockwell@gmail.com.

49374713R00086

Made in the USA
Middletown, DE
19 October 2017